Summer Mirrors

MICK BENNETT

Book III

Summer Mirrors

1

A T THIRTEEN, DEEP regret had not visited me, and although I remained naive to its malevolence until some years later, I felt its first pricks in the summer of 1955.

Most Saturday mornings that summer my father took us to Waterfront Ave beach to soothe his Friday night head, escort my sisters, and show his thirteen-year-old son how to ride waves. That summer magic happened. Magic that lasted through years to come. On Waterfront Ave beach I fell in love with salt water. I became aware of new and old, learned the difference between permanent and fleeting, and began to wonder about who I was.

The permanent happened early. Teresa married. Our house seemed so much larger. On the beach, Mary Ellen screamed everything brand new. At fifteen, she jittered constant embarrassment as she studied the faces of boys passing our blanket. Mary Jean at eight matched her complaint for complaint, except she didn't care about freedom from the old man's supervision. She wanted shade and snacks—I still picture her eating chips under our umbrella. Starving Albino Child, I called her—not in front of the old man, of course.

The year before, transistor radios became available. Now they began to appear on the beach. Ball games, music, and endless commercials kept time with the waves. A transistor radio was far beyond my family's means—the first ones cost fifty dollars—but the men lucky enough to own one shared one trait beyond a good salary: they showed off. How? Simple—they cranked the volume. They turned up Red Barber, *That grounder was slicker than boiled okra…*or Mel Allen, *That ball is going, going…it is gone!*

Women's bathing suits shrank right along with radios according to Mary Ellen. "There goes a bikini," she'd point out to father. He never had to girl watch. His daughter did it for him.

"Maybe next year," was the standard start of his reply that closed with, "I've told you before. Ask your mother."

Mary Ellen didn't give up—she remained relentless until she graduated from high school. By then, she'd put on a few pounds and kept to a one-piece anyway.

I had more important things on my mind. Besting my father in a race was the most important.

At high tide, he waded out thigh deep before diving under a breaker. At low or between tides he sprinted through the back wash and collapsed down into a wave just as it rolled toward its break. His legs seemed to vanish for a moment in the sand. Then as the wave broke and flattened out, he stood straight up, towering above the surface, up to his knees in the wash.

He knew Waterfront had a ledge, a sudden drop of swirling gravel and bits of shell deep enough for a headfirst dive at high tide or a head-up jump at low. After the ledge, unless there had been a serious storm or bottom shift due to unusually strong currents, Waterfront beach flattened out near the last barrel into a sand bar.

We local kids knew about it—not the Bennys, though. At high tide we would sprint straight out in the center of the swimming area between the ropes without fear. We knew once we swam out far enough, we could feel for the bottom. The water still over our heads, we'd grab a breath and go under, both arms up straight, to bounce up off the firm, sandy bottom. Sometimes at low tide, we huddled around the last barrel treading water—you couldn't sit on the rope—Casivette would whistle you off the second both cheeks touched coiled manila. Besides, by August the ropes had so much seaweed hanging on them, they were slick as snot.

To race my father, I had to do two things. First, I had to lose my friends. Hank Mariucci, Kenny Blalock and I weren't attached at the hips—we were attached by our mouths. Out swearing each other and insulting innocent strangers filled our beach days. I had to use an excuse to swim with my father— I had to piss.

Second, I had to convince him to race. I asked all the time. The poor man had a head the size of a watermelon, and I pestered the hell out of him. Usually after lunch, he gave in.

I knew how my father entered the water because I usually followed him after he toed a line in the sand, counted three, and said, "Go!" I knew I lost precious seconds letting him sprint ahead, but I enjoyed watching him run. He moved with the quickness of an athlete past his prime—without grace, but with the nimbleness of quick-twitch muscles still anxious to fire. I could run with my head down and still trail him by ten feet once we hit the water, so that didn't matter. Instead, I watched where he entered and determined a better, less crowded route to whichever barrel we selected for the race's finish. The contests always held that hope, that I would find an open path while he would be forced to circle a pod of gossipy ladies, their white bathing caps bobbing back in laughter.

I tried cheating. Since Casivette and his minions kept a close eye on the ropes, they were always free for me to pull myself out to the barrel. That strategy failed every time. My father turned for a breath on his right side when he swam a crawl except if we selected the north barrel. Then he'd breathe on his left, see me, sharpen his angle, and cut me off. I'd watch the soles of his feet as he pulled himself ahead of me, his laughter blowing spray off the surface.

I tried different strategies. In rough water, I bellied out to my chest before swimming as the lifeguards did when making a save. My father performed what he called a trudgen crawl. Instead of a flutter kick, as he lifted his head for a breath, his legs spread and snapped together in a scissor kick. It may not have been the fastest stroke in a pool, but when swells hit three or four feet, it kept him moving damn fast. I tried it. I didn't have his snap or long legs. I flutter-kicked my ass off. I dug my arms in and out of the water so fast, my head snapped back and forth, side to side as if I was eating corn on the cob in a cartoon. Nothing worked.

When he finished far ahead of me, I let hours pass between contests. Instead, when the sun burned midafternoon or the crowding of the blankets surrounding us got to me, I'd snap to my feet from the sand and ask, "Wanna ride a few?"

He taught by example. I saw how to dip a shoulder to go left or right—a necessary skill in a crowded ocean—how to catch the wave, to bail out. The old man showed off, no doubt about it. If he had room, he'd flip-turn in the shallows just as the crest slowed and stand up straight watching other riders slow to a stop in front of waders. More than a dozen times, I saw him turn away from shore and laugh when some kid bowled over a grandpa and caught hell from a guard.

That summer on the Fourth, we had some rough surf. The water tore away the bottom, and at high tide, we had some beautiful big breakers. There was a moon tide, and the waves rolled in from the third barrel and broke sharp and full at the second.

We raced, and I never made it past that second barrel. I caught a mouthful of water, hacked and spit. Treading water, my feet stretched for the bottom. It wasn't there. Another breaker caught me without a breath, and I panicked. I fought for the surface, made for the north rope, and pulled myself in.

From shore I saw the old man treading by the third barrel. He waved an arm for me to come out. I shook my head no. I didn't know if he had seen what happened. The fear of him realizing what I had felt, what I had done and why—it filled me up to my throat.

He swam in. I didn't wait for him. On the blanket, Mary Ellen waited until he returned before she said, "James got himself swamped by a big breaker."

"That so?" My father looked out at the water as he dried himself.

I stared at my sister, positive my hands could entirely encircle her throat. I couldn't say a word. Mother was along for the holiday, her middle beach appearance—Memorial Day and Labor Day the others. As usual, she read my mind.

She eyed me until I looked away from Mary Ellen. My father sat on his towel after shaking it carefully. He spread it down in alignment with the sun, stretched out on his back, fixed his hands into the sand at his sides, and closed his eyes.

Years later, I realized that Fourth of July was the last time I raced Dad. I could never show the slightest weakness in front of him.

A week later, Mother let me purchase a diving mask and snorkel with money saved up from my paper route. All the lifeguards knew my routine—carry the mask down to the water, rinse it out, spit in it, and wipe it clean. I'd stay face-down in the water, beyond or between the breakwaters, depending on the tide, for the rest of the day.

The bottom and its treasures held my attention the rest of the summer. I saw schools of spearing, tiny fish that darted this way and that as one. Blue crabs saluted me with raised claws as they crawled out from beneath my shadow. Horseshoe crabs—I loved to grab their spike tails, hold them out of the water, and listen to the Bennys gasp as the clawed legs pinched at air. I saw flounder, blowfish, and mackerel. Out by the second barrel in late July, a fish—probably a small sand shark—swam past so fast and turned so sharply I hugged that barrel waiting to feel teeth. Man, I needed getaway speed. I needed swim fins.

I asked Mother to share her bingo winnings with the family—no dice. These were my limbs, damnit. I shorted the *Asbury Park Press* until I had the cash, bought the fins, and gave them to Hank. He and his crewcut, braces, and cocky mouth would bring the fins to Waterfront beach. On Saturdays, when Father and my sisters joined me, Hank used the fins as his own—part of our deal. With ease, he would pull things off and then flash a silver grin to me— the only kid who could make braces cool.

In late August, Hank's family moved to Bloomfield. A little over an hour away on the Parkway. A thousand miles from the churned feelings and doubts inside me that summer. He visited now and then, carefree and unaware of the longing adolescent he had left behind. We were never as close.

A tidal change.

2

ON A SQUINTY-eyed afternoon a few days after Ronny taunted me and I opened up to Alice, I ended my day manning a gate way the hell south from my usual haunts. It was just after two. The southeast breeze swept over the sand doing its best to blow hotdog wrappers and tussle hair.

"Hello," I greeted the Barclay gate lady. A stern-faced woman with bad home hair color, she looked me up and down as if she wanted to fight me. We hadn't met.

"I hope you don't mind. I must mail this letter." She held it up, showing it to me as if it were the formula for eternal life. "I like to walk along Lake Como."

The post office is on F Street between Waterfront and Brady—five blocks west and two blocks south of Barclay. Instead of walking south to Waterfront or looking for a box on some corner, this woman, who probably topped out at a ½ mile an hour pace, planned to walk north, and take an extra hour just to stroll past Lake Como.

"I'm sure there's a box between here and F Street," I told her.

Nope. Off she sauntered. This woman didn't listen to any voice other than her own inner idiot.

Minutes later, a cloud squatted over the sun passing me into shade. I brought a hand down from my eyes and glanced north down the boards for that woman. I spotted Robin crossing Ocean Ave from Sussex, one block down. She glided smack between the white crossing lines, purposeful and steady. Her big bag slung over her shoulder, blue blanket tucked under the opposite arm, she made her way up the Sussex Ave ramp and headed north for my gate on Barclay—a torpedo coursing amidships of my heart.

For me relationships had been like politics—bad theater with a repetitious plot. The characters and scenery changed, but the plot stuck with black hats vs. white hats. Standing in my gate guard spot, I turned and faced the water. When I glanced toward Robin, her eyes locked on mine so tight I couldn't look away.

"Jimmy Hanlon. Don't you pretend you don't see me."

So I was a full name now. I turned, lifted my voice, my free hand, and my eyes. "Hello, Robin. Another gorgeous—"

"I don't have time for another of your stories." In my small gate space, she dropped her bag and blanket. "I came down here for two reasons. One, you'll be interested to know I don't believe it. Why would you spread a false story about Ronny with an underage girl? First the cancer story and now this. Your summer's been one long lie. Just know I love Ronny. I'd like to believe that we both love him. That we have a connection, a mutual concern, no? "Now," she folded her arms, "that's out. Two, you need to get to your oncologist for a check-up. You promised me you'd see your oncologist, didn't you?"

I nodded. Her tan glowed new on her face and bare arms.

"And?"

"Good afternoon," I greeted beachgoers. "Have tickets for me? Thank you, thank you."

I watched the family walk past and down the steps onto the sand—a mom, two young boys and two teen girls.

"Jimmy, I don't mean to sound harsh, but I want to clear the air."

"The breeze takes care of that. Ronny took advantage of that girl, whose name is Linda. Remember when he assaulted your friend Lisa? As for me I've loved men and I've loved women. Listening to my speech and a beach badge will now get you onto the sand."

She bent down, picked up her bag and blanket like they were two lost children, and headed south.

I was pissed at the post office walker and disgusted with Robin. For the next two hours and ten minutes—I timed that woman so I could write her an accurate, obscene letter—I sat there thinking about what Robin had said before I tried not to think about it by watching the sights.

One guy snuck his dog onto the sand. He lifted him over the storm fence, dropped him, and then ran on at Brady. I didn't care if the dog shit on the beach. The cops don't.

The Dog Lady came past. By late August, she looked as brown as her pooch. That or the dog's coat had thinned from all the sun exposure and exercise. I got a better than usual view of her. She slowed and turned right at my gate. Her calves were fat oranges in the middle. She wore her dog-dragging, belly bag-belt over bright purple top and satin shorts that matched her varicose veins. They covered her legs like twisted, crazy roads. Arms angled at ninety degrees, she pumped her manicured fingers fast enough to make a breeze.

Three kids on bikes rode past my gate, their towels flying like capes from around their necks. I didn't bother to try to stop them. Head tilting at his shoulder, a runner who had to weigh more than me struggled past. One arm hung limp and flapped like a broken wing. He hit the end of the boards, turned, and came back in more of a shuffle than a jog. Now the opposite arm dangled.

I watched the gulls. It was high tide—prime sand flea hunting. One circled over the group before making a flapping landing on its outskirts. A few of the ones already walking gave him warning or welcoming shrieks—I don't speak sea gull. They all scattered when the rule-breaking dog and his master ran along the shoreline.

All that watching didn't help. I heard Robin's words over and over. *Your summer's been one long lie.* If being a nurse exposed her to every emotional state of the human condition, how could such an intelligent woman who strove for health and well-being alongside suffering and death show such arrogance of certainty? *You can hate everyone you please, but not love everyone you love.*

When that Barclay gate woman got back, I looked at my watch. "Does your husband work at Kedersha's shoes?"

"No."

"I thought you might get shoes for free since you enjoy wearing them out."

"My husband passed."

"A break for him," I mouthed.

I realized walking up my front steps it had been weeks since I'd been to a bar. Not since the Palace, when I stemmed Ronny and Vinny, the pedaling pimps, and watched them ride their city ladies on handlebars back to the charms of the condemned aisle.

I stood on my porch and looked across the street at the beach. Estel's summer ghosts stood by—Robin and Ronny meeting, Peggy on Ronny's shoulders, Ronny dancing to "Sugar Magnolia" and the look on the face of that lead singer. Everywhere it was Ronny. I missed my friend, my bodyguard. He'd been my ticket back into life. Now he wanted his fee and a hell of a lot of interest.

And Robin. What good would it do to talk to her? I'd have to do it all at once. I'd have to get them all together—Alice, Robin, and Ronny—and tell them the whole story. Me, Denny, Avon, Sophie—everything. Hope for my Sea Girt family was a matter of time. I had the patience, and I doubted my new sexuality-according-to-Ronny would go past the summer bartender-lifeguard crowd. My little granddaughters would grow up, and times change.

But my Belmar bunch had only weeks to go. After Labor Day, I'd be out of a job. Linda would be back in school. Robin and all the rest would go home, and the town's gears would slow down to what clam diggers called locals' summer.

The season had stopped coasting toward an end. Robin's words threw a wrench in the spokes. Now when I looked across the street, I didn't see anything but a lot of people wasting time, waiting for Labor Day, summer's last bash. It felt as if I were waiting for something or someone to come by, sweep an arm around me, and take me anywhere else so I couldn't see Robin sing "Two Out of Three Ain't Bad" into her beer bottle mic or look down from my kiss in my kitchen on Lughnasa. She'd said my summer was a lie.

I got a shower, fixed myself a nice cool mug of iced tea—I brew my own, that instant stuff sucks—sat down and started writing a list.

This list ended up about a page and a half long—I have large handwriting—and at the top of the first sheet I wrote Things 2 say 2 Alice, Ronny, and Robin. But I didn't know where to start. Instead, I started to fix dinner—frozen crab cakes and a box of mac and cheese. Ten minutes later, a frantic female voice yelled my name up from the sidewalk.

The coming whirlwind stopped me from finishing the list. Eventually it grew and became this book.

3

IT WAS LINDA. Straddling her bike, her T-shirt wet over her bathing suit and a small white towel-scarf around her neck, she looked like a drowned WWI flying ace.

"You're not due for another hour."

"Nice to see you, too."

"Come on up. I made mac and cheese, and crab cakes are cooking."

She dropped her bike on the dried grass. The last few weeks rain had been scarce, and lawns were colorless except where little green islands of dandelions sat in a sea of pale cream.

She slammed my upstairs door with a boom that almost jarred me off my balcony chair.

"Sorry!"

She slammed the bathroom door, too. I got up and went inside. I looked at the doorjamb. "Christ," I mouthed.

A thin crack ran horizontally in the wood almost opposite the knob. I sat on the sofa with my iced tea. I thought about giving her hell when she came out, but I figured I'd better find out what was going on first. I heard the flush and waited.

I didn't follow my own figuring. "Did you windmill this son of a bitch shut?" I pointed at my door. "The jamb's cracked."

She stormed past me without looking up from the floor, opened the fridge, took out a Pepsi, and popped it. "I said sorry. What jamb?"

I walked to the door, opened it, and ran a hand along the jamb. "Right here. This piece of wood." She came over with big eyes and got close enough to lick where I'd touched.

"That's a jamb? I didn't know what you meant. A jam, I thought you meant like being in a jam. I'm in a jam, all right."

Her voice froze my spine. Five hundred things catapulted into my brain at once. "What kind of jam?" I said slowly.

"Nothing." She walked into the kitchen and lifted the lid off the mac and cheese. "Orange powder instant."

"Linda."

"I don't want to talk about it." She checked in the oven. "Previously frozen."

"Mrs. Paul doesn't do fresh." I came next to her and put a hand on her shoulder. "What's going on?"

She slowly twisted from under my hand. "It's just Margaret. Just her bullshit."

"Watch the language." I felt the chill lift.

"Class hasn't started."

I got both her shoulders and steered her for her usual chair for our lessons at the head of the table.

She collapsed down like she'd been shot. She swept an arm across the tabletop shoving magazines, pencils, and crosswords aside to make room for her chin to rest on both hands. "She's such a bitch. She has me coming in by nine. It's barely dark at nine. You're getting your body clock ready for school, she tells me. School starts soon. I hate her." She stared straight ahead, and then rolled up her eyes to me without lifting her chin. "She drinks and calls me names. Last night she told me I helped kill Antony. Me and that prick lifeguard."

"No. What did she say exactly?"

"I don't remember. She gets on rants. She drinks and then explodes. I don't want to talk about it." She jumped up and went into the kitchen. "She didn't say helped kill him. You and your prick lifeguard killed him. I said the same prick who bought you that necklace? Where's my Pepsi?" She hopped up.

I pointed to it. "How do you know he gave her a necklace?"

"Well, she didn't have it when he came over the other night, and she did have it after he left. When's this gourmet feast ready?"

"So it's your mother. That's the jam you're in."

"That and I missed my period."

I had the craziest thought. As soon as Linda said the word period, I heard my mother say *your penance*—one of her favorites. In elementary school, I failed a spelling quiz. That afternoon, I fell on my knee and gashed it open. I got three stitches. Mother's gaze sanctioned each one. Invisible permission to be a told-you-so smart ass. I didn't know how the hell it got back into my head, but I wanted it out.

"Come sit down," I pulled her arm at the elbow and brought her back to her chair. "Please tell me details," I sat in my usual spot. "Now first, I remember you saying to me the first night you were over here that you were taking birth control pills. Is that true?"

"You remember that? Yes but no."

"Please don't rock back in that chair." I put a hand on top of hers and she let the chair drop down. "What does 'yes but no' mean?"

"I was but I skipped. I skipped a couple days when I went to the hotel because I left my pack home. It was only two."

"Is that allowed?"

"Who was I supposed to ask?" she stood up.

I let her stomp around for a minute before I asked her, "Okay. How late are you?"

"Days."

"Two days, ten days?"

"Shit! You and Margaret! You sound alike, you know?" She folded her arms and stood at the balcony slider, looking out.

"Did you tell your mother you're late?"

"Oh, Lord no. Tell Margaret," she snickered. "That'll be the day."

"Buddy Holly."

"What?" she spun around.

"Buddy Holly. He sang the song "That'll Be the Day." He got the title from John Wayne in a movie." I smiled at her.

"How can you joke about it?"

"I didn't want to sound like your mother."

"Cheerleading tryouts are next week. I don't have time for this!"

I got up, went over to her, and gave her a big, long hug. I let go with one arm. "Okay. Maybe we need to get an e.p.t. kit."

"What the fuck—"

"Ehh."

She spoke softly, slowly into my chest, "What the heck is an e.p.t. kit?" When Sophie told me she was pregnant with Alice, all I could think of was you asked for it, pal. This is what comes with the territory. I even remember laughing at my pun.

"A pregnancy test."

"What's e.p.t.? Initials? They stand for something?" "I don't know. You want me to make a joke?"

"Sure."

"Extra Pepsi time."

"That's just dumb." She perked up. "So I can find out right away?"

"Yup."

"Tonight?" She skipped-hopped to my key holder on the wall next to the refrigerator, pulled off the Caddy's keys, dangled them and smiled, "Now?"

"Let's have something to eat first."

We sat there and picked for five minutes after I dished out the mac and cheese, slid the crab cakes onto a platter, and got some glasses with ice for our Pepsi. I reached for my voice to ask for the tartar sauce—that I made from scratch—but before I touched my voice to my throat, Linda stood up.

"Not hungry. You're going into the drugstore, right? Don't I have to pee in a bottle or something?"

"I don't know."

When we were sure Sophie was pregnant, I made her pee in a bottle and then added a spoonful of Drano. Word was if the pee turned black, it was a boy, and if it looked greenish blue—it was a girl. Sophie's turned black and I bought a boy's baseball mitt. That was the same day John Glenn blasted off in Friendship 7 and orbited the Earth three times.

At the drugstore, it took me a while to find what I was looking for. The cash register lady gave me a funny look when I put the test on the counter to pay for it.

"Anything else?" she looked at the register.

I had the urge to go to the men's aisle and bring back a few dozen packs of cheap condoms.

"Throw a couple of those Swisher Sweets in the bag," I pointed, "and this, too." I grabbed a fistful of Bazooka out of the bowl on the counter. The lady stared at me. She counted Bazookas off by twos and mouthed numbers every time she fingered two new pieces. I wanted to tell her I had a fifteen-year-old girl in my car who might be pregnant by a thirty-three year old son of a bitch with the responsibility of a dog, and that this girl had more cool and composure than you do counting bubble gum.

Linda's transition from panicked to rational continued on the ride home. She didn't say one word to me in the Caddy. She held tight to the rolled top of the drugstore bag with both hands even after I told her I'd bought her some Bazooka. She really blows great bubbles.

Back home she flew up the stairs so fast I'm sure she didn't hear me say, "Don't slam the door."

I heard her in the bathroom rustling around. I pictured directions being unfolded and spread wide atop the sink or her lap. I thought of something and knocked on the door.

"What?"

"Do you need a bottle or something?"

"What?"

"A bottle, a glass."

The door unlocked and opened fast enough to suck the hair from my head. "What? I can't hear you."

"Do you need something to pee in?"

"Everything's in the kit."

This time the door closed quickly right up to the jamb and then gently pinched shut before the latch turned. I sat down on the couch.

I'd read that the test took ten minutes. That was a long ten minutes. I couldn't know then that in less than forty-eight hours I'd be sitting in my oncologist's office waiting for my own test results with Linda's outburst still in my mind.

"Shit!" came from inside the bathroom. "Shit, shit, shit!"

There hadn't been enough time for the test to take. "What is it? What's wrong?"

Nothing. Then the latch turned, and the door opened. "Come see."

I looked at her eyes. No tears, no resignation—nothing—like she'd been watching water boil. Then she turned and pointed at the toilet. The little test stick, halfway between floating and sinking, sat in the middle of a few pee bubbles. We both inspected the toilet.

"You think it's worth fishing it out?"

"I don't think so. I have those hockey puck bowl cleaners." I lifted the lid and showed her. "They're just bleach, mostly. But I'm sure the test's shot."

"I was concentrating on putting the stick under my pee. I guess I pee harder than I thought."

"Wasn't there a test tube or something?"

"Jimmy," she handed me the kit's box, "read it. It's not a chemistry set anymore."

She was right. Stick technology. "That's one hell of a gimmick. Well, what do you want to do?"

"Flush it." Her voice blew up as she left the bathroom. "That's toilet's a jinx! First I puke in it, now this!"

I picked the thing out, dropped it in the scrap basket, and washed my hands. Then I remembered to flush. I went out to the kitchen, opened the fridge, and took out a beer.

"So, you up for another run?" I stood with my back to her, popping the Pabst.

"How late are drugstores open?"

I looked up at the clock. It was after six. Something told me they closed at six, but I wasn't sure. However long those thoughts took to go through my head were too long for her to wait for a reply, because before I finished pouring that Pabst, my door slammed. I heard her run down the stairs. I started to follow. After a few stairs, I thought who the hell are you kidding and went out on the balcony in time to see her pumping away, standing on the pedals, riding like hell down Mercer, around the corner onto Ocean Ave, and out of sight.

I sat down inside and puffed away. I held out my hands. They shook as if I'd sprinted a mile. All I could think about was Linda and Ronny. The more I thought, the madder I became. Not to sound dramatic, but I think I could have shot his kneecap and watched him kick.

Looking back, I should have tended to my own house first. Linda wasn't my daughter. It had been only a few days since I had been honest with Alice, and I hadn't spoken to her since. All the excitement with Linda distracted me. Those first days after I'd told my daughter might have been very important days.

I should have called Alice that night and spoken to her, maybe asked for a lunch date, for an opportunity to talk to her. I'm sure it was a shock for her. Daughters don't expect a father to keep secrets. Instead, I occupied myself with the immediacy of Linda's problem.

Like a lost night in a crowded summer bar, what played out right in front of me clouded the bigger picture.

4

LINDA AND I knew where one health professional lived in Belmar. I took a chance she was headed for Robin's. Riding down Ocean, I didn't see Linda, but I saw Robin's Honda in her drive.

Up the steps I went. The porch looked the same—hollow framed, stretched-fabric chairs with little plastic tables alongside. I looked up at that tired, scalloped awning, rust stains under its eyelets. The front door opened with a rush, and I damn near fell down the steps from the shock.

"Jimmy," Robin said, "I saw you pull up."

I put one hand on my knee. "You scared the shit out of me."

She opened the screen door and came out. "I thought you might be around tonight."

"Maybe we can start over from this morning." No, you need to find Linda, I told myself. I sat down. The chair frame fabric stretched squeaky tight.

Robin's eyes smiled as she brushed hair from her forehead. She puffed her cheeks and blew out a sigh. "I'd really like that. Don't move. I'll be back."

After a few seconds, Lisa called from inside through the screen, "Hi, Jimmy."

Two unidentified female "Hi, Jimmy," echoes—neither one Linda.

"Hello," I said. I doubted they heard.

Sitting there, I realized I didn't know what the hell I was going to say. I sure as hell wasn't going to mention Linda's situation. After all, how could my lie about her and Ronny get her pregnant? Shit spun around in my head faster than I could follow it. I got the feeling that porch was jinxed—every time I visited things went to hell.

Sure enough, Robin came back with a bottle of Chianti Classico—our old standby—and two glasses. My gut told me I didn't have time for wine, but what came out of my EL was, "Wow. My dinner party favorite."

"You bet." She handed me a glass and poured. "One rule tonight, Jimmy," she sat down.

All those thoughts spinning between my ears thirty seconds before smacked to stop in a giant chain-reaction pile-up. "Okay."

"No mentioning a certain person we both love."

"Ronald Reagan?"

"You're half right."

"Promise," I raised a hand. "So you thought I'd be around tonight?" I smiled to myself. Way to knock it into her court. She smashed an overhead winner.

"I counted on your new sense of personal responsibility."

I could smell it coming. Doctor talk over Chianti. Robin started in, and I instantly flipped my teacher's-talking switch I used all through St. Rose High School and every doctor visit over the last year. It was the only high school skill I still used in adulthood.

Dozens of medical terms and a glass of wine later—and I sipped—I started to nod my head and acknowledge over and over, "You're right, you're right," just so she would stop. I heard myself say my oncologist's name, his phone number, directions to his office, all the time wondering where Linda had gone.

"I'll call and make the appointment for you. I know you don't like to talk on the phone. Jimmy, I'll go along if you want. I'll even drive," she put down her glass, touched my arm, and laid those blue eyes on me.

I put my hand over hers. This fucking hole. I put down my glass and picked up my voice from my lap. I didn't want my hand to leave hers. "I'm off Thursday."

"Two days. Well, I'll hit his hospital office tomorrow morning after Shop-Rite. It's my turn to do the house food and booze shop."

"You're talking forty-five minutes from the Shop-Rite to Monmouth Medical. Don't go over lunch when the Fort lets out," I cautioned, helpful as always.

She didn't even finish her wine. She walked me to the Caddy and stood alongside while I fired up that big V-8. "Want a ride, little girl?" I smiled and did Groucho with my eyebrows.

Robin laughed. "Not tonight."

"Have plans?"

"Jimmy."

"I didn't mention any names." I put my voice down. I was done talking.

The top and windows were down, and I had my left arm gallantly bent over the door top. Soft as a breath she touched my arm. "I'm glad we got this done tonight."

Before I cruised the boards searching for Linda, I drove past Peggy's. She sat on her porch with a magazine in both hands. A cigarette burned in an ashtray. She didn't look my way. I waited for a few seconds. She kept her eyes on the magazine, reached over, and took a drag on her cigarette. I figured if Linda were home, they would have yelled something to each other by now, so I took my foot off the brake and just kept going.

Linda had a few places she hung out, and I coasted past them to get a better view. I crawled past the arcade, McDonald's, and the surf shop.

I thought I recognized some of her girlfriends outside the surf shop—the early evening place to meet for the high school set. I parked on Ocean heading south right in front of the place. I got out and walked up to it. Music and the smell of resin rolled out its open double door. Surfboards hung in the big front window like giant salami.

Inside there were surfboards on racks, surfboards against the walls, and two boards on work horses getting patched with fresh fiberglass by a long-haired, bleached blond kid. Three girls and one guy stood around the boards and watched this kid lay on fiberglass like a surgeon dressing a burn victim. He applied a strip, stood back, and examined it every which way before asking the guy, "Look okay?"

"Dude," the guy smiled and shook his head yes. Two of him could have fit in his baggies.

I may as well have been a small flying insect. I probably could have cleaned out the cash register. Nobody noticed me until one girl glanced up for a second. She whispered something to her girlfriend—not about me. Neither looked my way. They kept their eyes on the blond bombshell. I couldn't blame them—he was a beautiful kid.

The Commodore was two blocks down. Standing on the sidewalk outside the surf shop, I weighed pluses and minuses. As usual, logic took a back seat.

I walked up the stairs to the Engine Room. They should have renamed it the Fire Engine Room. It's hard to describe what water damage looks like if you've never seen it. The only thing I could think of was an old friend of mine describing his LSD experience—walls melting, colors mixing with other colors.

The bar and the floor looked okay, but everything vertical dripped, and the ceiling had a bad case of squeezed paint zits. The pool table was gone. A bunch of temporary plastic tables and chairs filled the lounge. Glade air fresheners sat in the center of every table. Four of them sat on each corner of the bar. Some were Sea Breeze, others were Pine. The Commodore couldn't make up its mind what it wanted to smell like instead of smoke. I could have saved the hotel money—twenty guys all smoking my anisette cigars would have created a permanent licorice atmosphere.

I went upstairs to the second floor. It didn't look too bad except in the corner where the fire had been. Same thing on the third floor. On the fourth where the fire started, they had half the hallway roped off in yellow cop tape. I went back down to the engine room. I wanted a drink before going up to the second floor again and knocking on that door. I sat at the bar. A pretty young bartender came up to me.

"Hi, what can I get you today?"

I looked at her. I knew I knew her. I didn't remember the face—she had a deep tan now and wore her brown hair back instead of long—but I recognized her perky voice. "Jameson, neat."

She smiled at me. "Is that a mixed drink?"

"Jameson," I pointed at the bottle, "the green one."

She turned around and found it. "Oh, the Irish whiskey. Okay, I gottcha." She brought the bottle to me and put it on the bar. "How do you want it?"

"Neat."

She laughed. She looked at the bottle like it would tell her what the hell I was talking about.

I smiled at her. "It's okay. I thought you'd know by now. It's almost Labor Day. You're Katie, aren't you?"

"Yes."

"Jimmy," I held out my hand. "We met back in June."

She held the bottle's neck with one hand, shook mine, and when she let go pointed, "Ronny's friend!"

"That's me."

"Oh my God, I remember you. That day Ronny and that guy—his mouth was all bloody. God, that was awful. That was my first day. What a way to start a job, right, Jimmy?" She poured me a damn half glass of Jameson. "And you said neat. I didn't understand you. Sorry. Sure, I remember you," she trailed off, walking down the bar to a man and woman who'd been rolling their eyes at our reunion. "Where's Ronny been hiding?"

"You haven't seen him?"

"They laid me off after the fire. I just got back on the schedule."

This was Katie who made Ronny late the day we took off for Florida. That seemed like—shit, I won't say it. It wasn't that long ago. Summer hadn't played a joke on me for several weeks. She caught up that night. I took a sip of Jameson. You've been letting me off the hook for a while, I thought. "She's making up for it," I mouthed.

"What Jimmy?"

"Katie, summer's playing tricks on me today. Can I take this upstairs?"

A sign right behind her read NO DRINKS OR BOTTLES UPSTAIRS.

"I don't care," she waved. "I have the rest of this week before I go back to Bethlehem."

"I promise I'll return it."

I left a five on the bar and took my whiskey up to the second floor. I didn't remember the room number, but I planned to knock on more than one door— every door on the west side—I remembered Linda had mentioned she couldn't hear the ocean at night because of the racket on B Street.

I knuckle-knocked on each door. First one—nothing. The second door had a handwritten paper tacked to it—the lyrics to the Stones' "You Can't Always Get What You Want." I didn't bother knocking—the Stones were too grizzled for Linda, and Ronny was about as philosophical as a roll of toilet paper. I got an answer from a girl in the third room.

"Chiclet, that you?"

I knocked again. Why I don't know.

The door opened. "You're not Chiclet." Hair frumpy, in gym shorts and T-shirt, she yammered, "My boyfriend Chiclet's across the hall in the showers. I thought you was Chiclet."

I bowed. "My apologies. Wrong room." I wish I could have snapped a picture of her expression.

Inside door number four I heard a rustling of feet on the floor after I knocked. A man's voice called, "Who is it?" More feet moved and voices hissed at each other. I moved on. The next rooms were empty—doors wide open.

Back downstairs the Engine Room shifts had changed. I recognized Katie's replacement—a guy from the old days. He'd been a bartender at every crappy dive around the shore for more than twenty years. Fat, mean, and crater-faced, puff-nose ugly, he wore enough gold around his neck to sink a sloop. But I'd promised Katie about the glass.

When he saw me, his eyebrows lifted. I walked to a table, set the glass down, turned and lifted a hand goodbye.

"Ho-lee shit. Look at this. Hey, Shameless! I heard you turned fanook."

The night's fruitless search and that Jameson sunk my eyebrows.

"Ho, don't tell me I hit a nerve!"

I stared right at him. "It's goin' around, Shameless." He held a cigarette between his fingers and flicked the filter with his thumb. He picked up a bar towel and started wiping.

"Maybe you started it."

"I heard it," he grinned, wiping. "Heard it more than once."

I plucked that glass I'd set down, brought it back behind my ear, and winged that baby as hard as I could at the space his head had just left. It hit the liquor shelf, glass flying everywhere. It wiped out one bottle. Two more rolled off the shelf and broke when they hit the floor.

"You crazy son of a bitch! Come back here!"

I was out the door and nearly down the stairs when I heard him one more time. I knew he wouldn't chase me. Every owner tells every behind-the-bar employee to never leave the cash register. Which also means never come from behind the bar. Besides, the fat, dough-faced bastard was probably the one guy in Belmar who couldn't have caught me.

The shakes were back big time. I kept both hands on the wheel and breathed deep to settle myself, but I still had to pull over into a diagonal space. I cut the engine. I would have paid ten bucks each for a cigarette and a cold beer.

"What the hell was all that about?" I mouthed out loud.

Headlights passed and filled the Caddy's interior with light. I'd let an idiot get to me. Lady Justice held up her scale. My side of the scale held the marginal. Ghost-like, we hovered above the pan and cast weightless shadows while the other side, packed full, sank flat to the ground. It never budged. Once people jumped on, they never stepped off. Friends who shared pews, Kiwanis, and martinis climbed aboard alongside the ignorant. Shoulder to shoulder they stood, collars buttoned tight against change, not a hint of clean, fresh air in the whole stinking bunch.

I parked right in front of my balcony. I turned off the Caddy and sat in the dark for a few minutes. Then I started to laugh. I hadn't thrown anything that hard since Babe Ruth League. And that bartender's mad moon face! I bent over, sucking air, held the steering wheel tight, and shook with laughter.

After I calmed down, I wiped my eyes and opened the Caddy's door. As I stepped around the bike standing on the sidewalk, a voice from above came to me.

5

WHATCHA BEEN UP to Jimbo?"

Ronny sat in the dark, feet propped up on the railing, a cigarette's glow illuminating his smile for a second.

"The prodigal lifeguard returns."

"This is what happens when you don't lock your door." He laughed.

I went up my stairs. The only light in the apartment came from the stereo. He had the Tops Greatest Hits playing low. For a second, I contemplated closing and locking the slider, so he'd have to jump one flight to get away.

"Did you find a beer for yourself?" I asked him through the screen.

"I brought my own. Six of the red, white, and blue ribbon, your favorite. There's three left."

I turned on the kitchen light and made myself a nice screwdriver. I thought about rolling a bone. At least it would stop me from killing him. If I had a gun...the thought crossed my mind. Which is why I don't own one. I took a deep breath and went out onto the balcony.

"So you've been here for three beers? Must be a pretty important reason for you coming here."

"I had two before I came so I could be sociable. Why don't you have a seat and relax, Jimmy?"

"Did you see Linda here?"

"Linda? Hell, no."

"She's usually here Tuesday nights for our lesson."

"I didn't come here to see Linda. I haven't seen Linda in weeks. Sit down, you're making me nervous."

"You want nervous? Linda was here tonight. We visited the drug store. I bought cigars, and she bought a pregnancy test."

It took until late August, but I finally said something to him he didn't have a smart answer for. I sat down, took one of his cigarettes, broke off the filter, and lit up.

"What did it say?"

"What?"

"The test, Jimmy, for chrissakes. Was it positive or negative?" He leaned forward and looked at me. I couldn't remember ever hearing such a concerned tone in his voice.

"We don't know."

"You don't know. Why is that?"

"Linda dropped the thing in the john. Before she read it, she dropped it."

"I don't know what you're talking about."

"It's a stick. The test's a stick you pee on and then wait ten minutes to read."

"And she dropped the stick in the john."

"Yes."

"I'm out," he shook his empty can and got up. "You want anything?"

"A gun."

He laughed. I watched him in the kitchen. He lifted my vodka bottle, took a two-bubbles pull, then opened the fridge, got a Pabst, and chased the vodka. He belched and then came out.

"She dropped the test in the john. Why didn't somebody just pick it out?"

"Because the test was compromised."

"The test was compromised. Why?"

"Because of the bleach tablets I use in the john."

He stood up and lowered his voice. "So you don't know, for whatever reason, if Linda is pregnant or not pregnant."I shook my head yes and lit another of his cigarettes from the first.

"I thought you quit."

"Someone got me started."

"So why didn't you get another test?"

"Linda left. It must be this apartment. Without warning, people I'm fond of bolt out of here."

He sat back down. "And you've been out looking for her."

I snapped my fingers and pointed at him.

"But you didn't find her. Look, Jimmy. I told you once, and I'll tell you again. One time. The night we left here. There's no way she's pregnant by me. Not unless my boys can swim through lambskin."

"You're a liar."

"No," he laughed, "I'm not this time. You heard me bragging to Vinny or whoever. It was all brag, Jimmy. And then you turned around and told everybody and their mother about what you thought, about what you believed. You should be the last fucking person to do that, you know? Yeah, I told people about you and Key West. I was pissed. Have you ever asked Linda about any of this? You ever ask her straight out about her and that Antony kid?"

"That dead Antony kid. The one you killed."

"Whoa, asshole! What the hell?"

"Why did you come over here?"

"I followed someone's suggestion. I'm regretting it more and more. Don't smoke so damn much," he snatched his cigarettes off the tray table. "You want to go look for her? Linda?"

"Whose suggestion?"

"You were at Robin's place tonight so take a guess."

"Between the two of you…"

"Hey, she's your best friend if you don't know it. You want to look for Linda or not?"

"Just what the hell did you tell Robin to convince her you're a good boy? Did you take her to Lakewood to meet mommy? A pilgrimage to respectability."

"I'll look for her. Did you try Peggy's?"

"Go there. Maybe you can do mother and daughter at the same time."

He went inside, and I heard my door close, and his footfalls go down the steps. He pedaled down to the boards and headed south.

After two good drinks and a bone, I was ready for bed. Summer had kicked my ass good and proper. She wasn't done.

I woke up twice. Once when the phone rang. It was Robin.

"You're all set. One o'clock on Thursday. You want company?"

"I do those things better alone."

"Don't skip it. I had to pull strings."

The second time at about two o'clock I got up to pee and get some ice water. I sat on the john—I don't turn on the light, and I refuse to stand up just to miss—and I suddenly remembered what Linda told me her mother had said, that Linda killed Antony. I'd said the same thing to Ronny. Me saying the same, cruel thing as Peggy—and meaning it—that jarred the shit out of me.

The next morning, I reported to my first relief at Annie's gate. As I talked to her a cop car pulled up parallel to the boards. It was straight out of 21 Jump Street. I'd never even watched the show. I knew it from the ads.

Two plain clothes not old enough to shave climbed out and came over to me.

"Jimmy Hanlon?"

"Guilty."

"This is for you." He handed me a summons. For a second, I thought his partner might tell me to have a nice day.

"Oh." Annie looked after them.

I read out loud. "A complaint has been filed…Kelway Enterprises…You must appear without fail on the following charges…" Kelway Enterprises—Will Kelly. That's great. That's two weeks' salary for one glass and three bottles of booze made in Newark."

A car pulled up and honked. "Oh, there's my ride." Annie put a hand on her hat, slung her thermos over her shoulder, and headed for her ride.

"Maybe I'll just mosey over to Mr. Kelly's house after dark and do my Earnest T. Bass imitation." That's what I told Annie at the end of the day.

"Didn't he throw rocks through windows? You don't want to do that. When is your court date?"

"The tenth."

"Of September."

"My favorite month. Surgery and fines."

Annie packed up her bag of cross-stitch, magazines, and chilled fruit juice. She shook her head and laughed. "Jimmy Hanlon. Tossing glasses at your age."

"It's not funny. Amusing, but not funny. Hey, don't forget my post-Labor Day party. We'll be free—at least most of us. What better time for a celebration than after we've broken the chains of servitude?"

"Oh, fine, Jimmy. Are you on tomorrow?"

"No. I'll probably see you Friday. I wish I'd see you tomorrow instead of Dr. CT Scan and his needle-sticking hordes."

She didn't say a word. She planted a soft smooch on my cheek just as nice as could be and took off.

There wasn't much of a crowd down at the north end of town. Empty diagonal spots along the boards looked like vacant school desks during flu season. South beaches were packed, probably with kids getting in summer's last licks. No doubt somewhere down there my talisman stretched out on her blanket, maybe Lucky under her head, unaware Uncle Jimmy stood alone blocks away losing his mind.

So this is what you missed, I told myself. This is what a teenage daughter can do to you.

The summer Alice was eighteen I lived in Pacific Grove just outside Monterey. My postcards from California were her favorite—all kinds of exotic flowers and plants in the middle of winter. I sent her a piece of kelp. I wrote, "Imagine this stuff dozens of feet long, and the surf chock full of it. The water's cold, barely sixty degrees, and dress on the beach ranges from bikinis to bulky wool sweaters."

She wrote back, "I love the rocks in the middle of the beach and water. I can imagine the spray lifting off them when a wave breaks."

Alice wasn't Linda. Twenty Alices wouldn't have put me through anything like one Linda in the eight or so weeks since we met. I kept looking south, searching between moving traffic along Ocean Ave for her bike, for that towel wrapped around her daredevil-pilot neck.

Most days Linda came by around lunchtime. No matter what shift I worked, I always had somebody's lunch break covered. She rode behind the diagonally parked cars. It drove me crazy. Backing out of a space, some old bastard or young kid driver looking in his rearview for oncoming cars along Ocean Ave would never react fast enough to stop for her when she rode north. Sometimes I'd see her coming. She pedaled like somebody was after her, eyes scanning the boards instead of looking straight ahead.

"Why don't you ride on the other side of Ocean?" I'd ask her.

She'd work on her gum, a chew a second, smile and shrug.

Still prime sun and surf time when I got home, I got a quick bite and headed south for the teen beaches. I hit each gate and every half-way spot between. Anything I thought I recognized—a girlfriend, a familiar bathing suit—I kept an eye on. If Linda didn't show for a few minutes, I took a walk down the sand to get a better look. I talked to two of her girlfriends and one guy I saw her talking to once. They all knew me. Hell, most of the local beach-going teens had asked to try out my voice.

With Seaside—the street Vinny lived on—being about the last kid-popular beach, I decided to take a stroll. Vinny's place—for all I knew still Vinny's and Ronny's—was just past B Street. I remembered walking to it along B after the Commodore fire. Nobody should have been home at that hour of the afternoon unless one of them took lunch and rode his bike from Loch Arbour. I couldn't picture Vinny doing that with Allenhurst Beach Club and cold Heinekens just a short walk down the shoreline.

I found the house Vinny lived behind and started walking down its driveway. I stopped halfway, remembering a garage apartment behind a private home with a ground floor entrance. I didn't remember empty boxes, ripped-open Pabst cartons, and garbage bags stuffed with humping flies—a trash obstacle course. I almost knocked on the back door of the house to ask if anybody had bothered to notice the mess.

No bikes in sight—I figured the apartment was empty. Just for the hell of it, I waded through the soon-to-be landfill to the entrance and tried the knob. It twisted open. Maybe they'd moved out. In late August, skipping rent is a popular pastime. I poked my head inside to check the stairs. They were free of clutter. One look back at the house—nobody was home there, either, from what I could tell—and I stepped inside, closed the door softly behind me, and stood in the darkness.

Eyes adjusting, a thought popped into my head. Just what—more accurately who—had me trespassing in a rat trap in the middle of a summer afternoon to find a fifteen-year-old girl? Robin's words came back to me—a mutual concern. After Antony Silva, I'd lost what I'd felt for Ronny that night way back in June at Estel's when he danced with Robin.

If I could find Linda and hear her side of the story, Robin could be proven right. And though I'd be proven wrong, the earth's axis might self-correct its tilt. Summer wouldn't end.

I stood inside the door. Music, radio music, I guessed, came from upstairs. Might as well climb the stairs. Halfway up, before my eyes moved to floor level, I heard something more—a rustling. Then an awkward thud on the floor. I took one step at a time. The rustling became regular. I saw the TV with the same wire hanger, aluminum foil antenna; two closed doors, the bathroom door open. The noise, of course, came from Ronny's room.

Then the rustling began to feature female accompaniment. It reminded me of a higher-pitched Oompa-Loompa song—the one from *Willy Wonka and the Chocolate Factory*. Every so often, the oompas became a voice that hissed urgent directions.

I should have turned around, gone down the stairs, and waited for somebody to come out of that hell hole. Instead, I stood there. It wasn't long before I recognized Peggy's voice, so I sat down to wait.

The place still smelled like piss. After the oompas and directions stopped, the voices became clear over the radio. Ronny came out first. He had on his rowing shorts and carried his Loch Arbour sweats in one hand and a cigarette in the other. He looked at me, stopped dead still, and smiled.

"How long you been there?"

"Two seconds."

"I'll bet." He hurried from one corner of the room to the other. "Peggy, where the hell's my boat clip?" He carried his keys and guard whistle on a brass boat clip—some people call them suicide clips.

"I don't know," came from the bedroom.

"Jimmy's out here."

"Jimmy who? Jimmy? Your Jimmy?" She came out. She had on white shorts and a tube top. Her finger and toenails were blood red, and she'd lightened her hair. It was wild, sticking out in all directions like Medusa's snakes. "How long—"

"Two minutes. Come on, I'm late. I don't want a sit down with Mrs. G. Ah-hah!" he snatched up his boat clip from on top of the fridge.

"Let me grab my suit." Peggy ducked back into the bedroom and brought a beach bag with her.

"You coming?" Ronny put a hand on my arm, squeezed hard and winked at me. "You want a traveler? I'm grabbing one." He opened the fridge and took out two cans of Pabst.

"Love those red footprints on the refrigerator door." I stood up. Watching Peggy leave, Ronny put a hand up to my chest to stop me from following her.

"I'll start the truck." Peggy pulled the car keys from her bag.

"We're right behind you." Ronny waited until she was all the way down. "Don't tell me. You're here looking for Linda."

I just stared at him.

"Don't say anything about Linda in the truck to Peggy. She hasn't seen her either. She drove to fucking Loch Arbour looking for her and made me come back here with her."

"She made you, huh?"

Now he rushed me down the stairs. We walked to a shiny red pick-up parked just down Seaside—a recent model Ford F-150. Peggy sat in the driver's seat. Ronny opened the door and held out his hand. "You get the hump, pal."

"Hah!" Peggy pulled out before Ronny shut his door.

"Christ!"

"You said you were late."

Peggy fiddled with the radio until she found a song she liked. I didn't recognize it. "How do you like my new wheels, Jimmy?"

"Very nice. I didn't think you were a pick-up kind of woman. An '86?"

"It's an '85. And she picks me up all the time."

"Hah-hah. He bought it, Jimmy. He should know."

"It looks like the '86." So I was riding in the bribe-mobile. "Shit just keeps piling up," I laughed.

"What?" She shifted gears like a pro.

"That garbage truck." I pointed. They both looked. It worked.

Peggy turned down the radio. Her leg next to me jiggled back and forth on the seat. "So are you coming by tonight?" She leaned toward Ronny and against me as if I wasn't there.

Ronny looked out the window. "I thought you wanted to look for Linda."

At a crosswalk full of beachgoers, Peggy slammed on the brakes. "You could help me look, damnit!"

"I'll help."

I lifted my voice to my throat to speak, but Ronny crossed his right leg up and over his left and knocked a heel hard into my knee cap. It hurt like hell, and I let out air.

"Hey, sorry. Little cramped with three in the cab."

His leg burnished, shiny with oil, his foot covered with sand flecks, I couldn't help thinking summer was playing tricks two days running. Nobody spoke the rest of the way. They dropped me home, and I picked up the Caddy and followed them.

At Loch Arbour, Ronny pointed to a spot close to the office, and Peggy pulled in, gravel flying. Both climbed out and left their doors open. They didn't wait for me. They hurried toward the gate like runners at the finish line.

I stood next to the open passenger door for a second before I reached over and opened the glove compartment. The flap dropped down, and I pulled out an envelope filled with those new-car papers you sit there signing after buying a vehicle. There weren't any — no temporary registration, no folded window sticker, and no sales copies. Just a signed rental agreement. The signature at its bottom read Ronald Hopkins.

I smiled, closed the glove compartment, and both doors.

Mrs. G flew around the office corner decked out in lime green kerchief and shorts, white top, socks, and sneakers.

"Ronny, I—and Jimmy! How are you, doll?" She went past Ronny, came right up to me, and gave me a hug. "Where have you been? We've missed you."

"I'm a working stiff, Mrs. G. I'm a Belmar gate guard."

"Wonderful. Wait'll I tell Darlene." She leaned back and looked me over. "You have color on your face." She put a hand on her cheek, "I just get burned." Then she ran after Ronny. "Ronny, may I see you a minute, dear? In the office, please, Ronny."

Mrs. G led Ronny into the office. I walked right past Darlene. Head down, busy with paperwork, she never looked up. Peggy walked ahead of me. She had a blanket and umbrella set up maybe twenty feet behind the stand. I watched her pack up. She folded shut her umbrella, tucked it under an arm, held her blanket at a corner and dragged it behind her up the beach to the gate. Head up, eyes straight ahead, her butt sported an exaggerated wiggle.

There were still a lot of people on the beach and in the water. It was low tide, and groups of kids stood waist-deep, watched for waves, and then ducked under, whooping it up. On the sand just north of the boardwalk, chaise lounges formed a circle and men poured and passed white wine in plastic stemmed glasses.

I walked in front of the stand. Paulie swept his black tsunami hair with an open hand and smiled down.

"Look who's here." He dropped his butt to the footrest and reached down a hand. "The man himself." His hair looked so much longer. Then I realized he had a center part, a double tsunami.

"Hello," I smiled up at the big Greek kid. "How's Teddy?"

He looked down. "Ted."

"Where's Vinny?"

Paulie smiled, touched his chin to his chest, then with both hands running up and over his forehead showed his face to the sun. "In the condemned aisle best we can figure."

"How long does it take to get laid? Fucking asshole." Ted looked around, behind, then up the beach toward the office. "Where the fuck's fearless leader? That woman he left with came back and she's leaving."

"The two of them brought me along."

Ted looked at his watch. "Past three and I haven't taken lunch yet. I'm takin' a swim." He sprang out and down. Sand flew from his landing, and his head pitched forward. Tree-trunk legs pumped to get ahead of his ass as he wheeled down the tide rise, arms pumping. He almost plowed over an old couple walking north before he got himself stopped.

Paulie gave him a round of applause and cupped his hands before yelling, "For Ted's next trick…"

After a minute, I saw Ronny. He came straight for the stand, his toes-first, choppy steps avoiding blankets, kiddie pools, and coolers.

He took a towel off the stand, wiped the sweat from his face, and looked around. "Where is Fontana? Why is Ted in the water while you're alone on the stand?"

"An hour ago, Vinny—"

"Don't bullshit me, Paulie. I just got my ass reamed by that psychotic woman. Payback is in order."

"Vinny's in the condemned aisle."

Ronny looked toward the club. Mrs. G fired around a corner, shooed some locker boys away from the silver pipe railing, and stopped in front of the gate leading to the condemned aisle, hands on hips.

"Oh, fuck, no. Don't go in there. Is she saying something, Paulie?"

"Can't tell, skip."

"Don't do it…"

Mrs. G reached a hand down to the gate latch and pulled it open just as Vinny came out, a towel over one shoulder. He smiled at her and nodded as if she'd handed him a diploma. She closed the gate and walked toward the main lockers, clapping her hands after Mark the locker boy.

Halfway to the stand Vinny saw me and pointed. He smiled at Ronny. At the stand he stopped, yawned, and stretched. "Oh, mutha fucka, mutha fucka."

Ronny watched Vinny peel and hang his sweats. He hung the sweatshirt by the hood and spread the pants on a support beam, straightening and fussing. Ronny kept watching.

"Hey, Ralph Lauren. Where you been?"

"Where you been? I've been here. Somebody hasta rescue Ginny and Mary. They're trapped in my locker."

"You know what old lady G said about girls being back there."

"That's why they're stuck. We heard Mrs. G on 'er way in. So I came out and they stayed hid. They're fine." Vinny climbed up on the stand. "They got weed."

Ronny looked at Paulie. "It does no good to talk to him."

"Where's that woman?"

"Which woman would that be, Vinny?"

"Peggy. She find her daughter? You fuck her?"

"No. We drove to Monmouth Mall and shopped for parasols."

"If you had Linda at our place, you're the dumb ass."

It frightened me to hear Vinny make sense. I'd gotten myself into this organized grab-ass again, and I wasn't happy about it.

Ted came to the stand.

"Take off, Teddy. Be back before Glinda leaves at five in her bubble."

I looked up at Vinny. "I got a summons this morning. Destruction of private property at the Engine Room."

"What'd you do?"

"I brought the cheese with a bar glass."

"You what?"

"He used a glass for a fastball, Vinny." Ronny smiled at me. "You're getting younger by the second. So you were all pissed off after last night, and then this morning, you came looking to bust my ass."

"Just looking for Linda. I had no idea you'd be at your deluxe accommodations early in the afternoon."

"Yeah, well. Neither did I. So you still don't know where she is. Linda, I mean."

"Nope. But you're helping me look for her after you get off today. You and Vinny."

"What'd I do?"

"Nothing yet." I motioned for Ronny to follow me a few steps away from the stand. "I'll give you two a lift home after work. Maybe you can help me look for Linda on some Belmar beaches."

"Or else what, Jimmy?"

Ronny stared at me. The wind blew his hair all crazy as he smiled the biggest, widest, fuck-you smile I ever saw.

"Or else Peggy is going to see this two-week rental agreement," I produced the paper from my pocket and held it up, flapping in the breeze, before I tucked it safe away. His smile gone, he moved to the stand and climbed up. He sat between Vinny and Paulie.

"Stick here, Vinny. Don't move. Unless someone's drowning, don't move. And don't let me move."

A southeast, chilly wind and clouds settled in for the late afternoon. Beachgoers are like eighth inning fans—they see somebody pack up to leave and try to beat them. By four-thirty the water was empty. I didn't have a towel or blanket and damn near froze. All this because of a goddamn slippery pregnant test.

When Mrs. G's Lincoln pulled out of the lot a little after five o'clock, Ronny gave a little whoop. He sat between Vinny and Paulie on the stand. I sat on the bottom step.

"Maybe we'll hit the Palace on the way home. You boys up for it? My treat."

"I could use a belt or two," Paulie said.

Vinny agreed. "Captain's treat."

"Settled," Ronny said. "All of us fine-looking lifeguards in our shorts. You're coming along for that, aren't you, Jimmy?"

I stood up and faced him without saying a word. If Linda were pregnant, the child couldn't be his. I told myself that over and over. Not even Ronny could be an asshole with that hanging over his head.

"I'll take that as a yes." He turned and looked at the entrance. "Here comes Teddy. You two lock the boat up, Vinny. Let's wrap this day up."

Vinny carried the wooden roller over to the boat and waved Teddy over to help. A good, strong southeast breeze crossed the beach. Ronny sent Paulie to grab the trash can liners before the locker boys finished their clean-up. Three of them wandered around poking crab nets underneath trash. Ronny packed up the stand—first aid kit, line buckets, torps.

The snack bar had closed tight at 4:30. Mr. and Mrs. P were probably sitting down to whatever they drank before dinner. I figured Mr. P for a beer man. Mrs. P probably sipped anisette.

By 5:45, everything was done. The beach looked like I felt—done for the day. Just a few hardy souls dressed and ready to go home milled around on the boardwalk to catch a last ocean breath. But my day was far from over.

With nobody in the water, Ronny and the others guards sat on the stand's bottom step out of the wind—it's amazing how much faster air moves eight feet up off the beach. I huddled in a blanket Mark the locker boy brought me. We were close to being pals—maybe because lifeguards picked on us. I stood up and started to hop around to keep warm before I remembered the lifeguard shack and headed up there.

It was the first time I went into it. The guards kept personal things in the condemned aisle. Their shack was for storage—oars, lines, extra barrels. Barbells, iron weights, and a long wall mirror occupied one wall. An 8x8 sheet of plywood gave some privacy to a mattress on the floor in a back corner. A couch with cinderblocks for rear legs sat opposite the weights and mirror. Someone had chopped a crotch-high hole in the north wall. Guards had written their names and summer years on the inside walls. The earliest year was 1971. That meant 16 years in a row a nor'easter didn't sweep the shack out to sea. Standing all the way west next to the street didn't hurt its chances of survival. Someday, though, its luck would run out along with the whole damn beach club. Sitting north of a long jetty isn't the best place to be in a nor'easter.

I was so restless I couldn't stand it. I went out to the Caddy. I passed Darlene closing the office. She had most of the shutters lowered already—I thought to keep the wind out. I looked in under an open shutter and caught a locker boy and Darlene playing doctor. He saw me, adjusted his shorts, and flew out the door.

Darlene blushed, "Have a good one, Jimmy."

She dropped the shutter and disappeared. I heard the lock latch.

In the Caddy I smoked a cigarette—I'd bought a pack thinking about my doctor appointment tomorrow. Scan techs and my oncologist. I sure as hell didn't look forward to that. I rubbed my throat under my ear and felt the tenderness. I'd been waiting for a sore throat or fever. My throat felt fine, and my temp read normal.

The next day I visited the clinic. I won't go into details. You know how it turned out. Within hours, I received results of my scan, a recommendation for immediate chemotherapy and radiation treatments, two appointments at two different cancer centers, and a bright red cocktail served with a fruited sword, yellow paper umbrella, and blue plastic straw that I ordered at Evelyn's Tiki Bar & Restaurant.

But I'm getting ahead of myself.

7

PATIENCE—NOT ONE of my strong points. I had no plans of letting Ronny out of my sight. The idea of finding Linda had grown in my head every second of every minute that afternoon. Now it suddenly found unexpected company. I had to see for myself if Ronny could remain so callous, if his colossal apathy was real. Disgust and fascination filled me as I watched him walk his bike to the Caddy. He moved in slow motion. It was as if I was watching the crane lift the white Mustang out of Shark River Inlet.

We looked like July. Bikes packed in the Caddy's trunk, the lid tied with yellow beach cord, we cruised down Kingsley with the radio roaring. Ronny sat in front; Vinny, Paulie and Ted crammed in back. I found a spot right outside the Palace, and we poured through the open garage doors and up to the bar.

A group of Asbury guards in their red gear leaned against the opposite end, girls and couples sat at tables. The jukebox had traveled from its old spot. Now it sat across from the opening of the service station, so the bartender had easy access. Every time it died one of the tenders fed it back to life.

Shots of Stoli and beers all around.

"Fuckin' August," Paulie toasted.

Teddy left us for the Asbury crew. More red shorts and sweats came into the bar. Ronny ordered another round, and I lost track of Teddy. A minute into Southside Johnny, the jukebox jumped. An Asbury guard—not a big kid by any means—had shoved Teddy's double-wide ass and plastered the music against the wall. Everybody looked over. The two grappled, pushed, and wrestled their way onto the floor holding each other's sweatshirts—a horizontal hockey fight. The bouncer and one bartender rolled them out through one of the garage doors, and two girls on the sidewalk walked around them, pointing down, laughing.

"Don't make me call the cops!" screamed the behind-the-bar bartender.

"C'mon, Teddy! I mean Ted!" Vinny cheered, but no orange L.A. shorts hurried to help.

The Asbury guards spurred their guy too. None of the guards moved. Neither of the rollers was serious. Not a fist or elbow was thrown—just grabbing and pulling fabric.

Before they let go of each other and got up off their knees, puffing like schoolboys, I noticed Ronny. Facing the Asbury guards, he stared straight at one apart from the group—I didn't know the guy. He didn't turn around to check Teddy and his skating partner. He kept a bead on that one guy—the biggest Asbury guard there.

Teddy bent over, sucking wind. He took off walking south.

"Hey, Big Ted!" Paulie called.

"Wunderbar!" Teddy called back.

Paulie nodded at us and followed him.

"They're gone," Vinny said. "Teddy rolls good."

The Asbury guard got backslaps and laughs from his brother guards. He wasn't much bigger than Paulie, weight-wise. He'd taken Teddy's sweatshirt, pulled it down at the shoulders and bear hugged him to a draw—worth a beer and congrats in his mates' eyes. No words passed between red and orange-clad warriors.

So the Three Stooges climbed into the Batmobile and headed south. I'd been patient long enough.

"Time to help me find Linda," I told them riding down Kingsley. Neither spoke a word until we crossed the Inlet Bridge into Belmar.

"We lookin' in a bar?"

Old stone face didn't crack a smile at Vinny's joke. He sat next to me, smoking, flicking the ash over the door top. When I passed my place, he looked down the street. I pulled over and parked on the west side of Ocean Ave.

"Vinny, you're out here. Check the beach from here to Monmouth. I'll meet you at the Commodore. Drinks and bones are on me."

I pulled into traffic. The radio played 101.1 oldies. WCBS FM sang the jingle. Cousin Brucie called us cousins, spun the first five notes of

"Satisfaction," and crowed, "It's summer and seven o'clock in the greatest city in the world!"

"Where you dropping me, Jimmy?"

"Have any place in mind?" I kept one eye on the car ahead of me—a Buick, so probably some old geezer—and one on the boardwalk.

"You can pull over any time you like."

Two mommies pushed babies in the crosswalk. Brake lights blinked. "I'm stopped."

"You're in the line of traffic."

"You can't hop out, Hoppy?"

"I can. But I'm not. I need you to pull over."

Cars moved again. Two more blocks of stop and go. He leaned back, spread his legs wide, and draped his left arm over the seat top.

"Lots of traffic for a weekday."

"You want out here? You can check the Commodore."

"And where will you go? Sussex, maybe?"

"I'm not thinking about Robin right now."

We passed Monmouth. "The saving grace for you is that you always put your voice in your right-hand pocket. Everything else goes in the left-hand pocket. Otherwise, I could reach over and snag that rental paper."

The boardwalk pulsed with people.

"I bet if I grabbed for it—"

But he grabbed my right wrist and twisted my hand pinkie up. The air whooshed out of me, and I hit the brakes. Two seconds later horns exploded.

"Can't stop here!" Ronny laughed. He let go, picked my voice from its pocket, and dangled it in front of my face. "What? I can't hear you with the horns blowing."

Cousin Brucie talked about shaving cream as I waited for the pain to quit.

"Okay," I mouthed.

"No take-backsies."

He dropped my voice into my lap after I took the rental form from my pocket and handed it to him.

"Going to turn and look in the Tropical? Hang a—nope. Too late," he turned his head. "Passed it by. Just like your summer, Jimmy. Passing you by. What, you got a week and a half left? Then what?"

"I'm U-turning at the end of town."

"So? That mean I don't get to jump out to look?" He tucked the registration down into his rowing shorts. "Maybe I shouldn't put it there." He smiled and snapped the elastic on the short's waistband. "After your U-turn, then what, Jimmy? Look at the line outside Ray's," he pointed. He leaned at me, smiling. "I'll tell you what. You'll be back in your apartment again, squawking to strangers miles away over your radio. No more Robin, no more job. Just who do you think's going to want to come see you? You're a fucking pariah."

Pariah or no, voiceless or not, I have sharp eyes. I didn't look at the bar line. I looked at the boardwalk, and there on a bench facing Ocean Ave sat three girls. I didn't recognize the bookends, but I sure as hell knew the tomb between. The damn traffic picked that second to move.

I was headed south—traffic bumper to bumper both ways—driving an aircraft carrier, watching those girls getting smaller and smaller in my rearview.

I waited until I had two car lengths ahead of me. Then I whipped the wheel right, gave the Caddy some space to turn, and pulled her nose into the northbound lane. Horns blared like crazy. I went into Yankee Stadium exit mode—inch ahead, ignore the horns, and hope the other driver likes his car more than you like yours.

"What the hell are you doing?"

I kept inching the Caddy forward until she straddled the double yellow line. The driver of the car that wouldn't let me in made eye contact—a big no-no in the Bronx. I smiled, and he waved me in as I kept an eye on those three monkeys down the boards.

I wasn't alone.

"See ya," Ronny laughed getting out. He jumped up onto the boards and jogged straight for the girls.

When I saw an open diagonal parking spot, I pulled into it, cut the engine, and opened my door. Ronny had half a block on me. I watched the bastard stand still after Linda spotted him. She ran to him. I kept walking. She kept hugging him, her head tucked, heels lifting. A beautiful breeze puffed me the good news.

"I got the vapors; I got the vapors," she repeated into his chest. Her arms came up around his neck, and he whispered something to her.

Then he turned, brought her around with him, smiled at me, and said, "Found her."

In the flash of his smile, I knew there would be no reckoning. No mother, cop, or ASL tutor would knock away that triumphant summer smirk. But my compass self-corrected. Linda was safe. She beamed at me, and summer's dazzle rolled like a big slider whooshing up the sand at my beach chair giving me no choice but to jump up laughing.

My eyes glued onto hers. Our arms opened, and I bent down on one knee and welcomed her with an Al Jolson hug and smile.

"Woo-hoo!" Fists straight up and clenched, her flip-flops slap-slapping the boards. "I got the vapors, Jimmy!" She squeezed me tight around my neck.

"Don't cut off his air," Ronny came close to us. His eyes never left me. "You said drinks and bones are on you. See you at the Commodore. Don't be long."

8

LINDA WATCHED RONNY walk away.

"Where have you been? And what does Ronny know about you being pregnant? Answer the second question first."

"But I'm not pregnant. Oh, I don't want to hear that word again till I'm fifty."

She had a towel wrapped around her waist. I could see her nipples through her wet, bright yellow bathing suit top and thought wrap the damn towel around all of you.

"Can we sit down?" I motioned at a bench.

"Gotta say bye to Ashley and Jill."

Hands holding her towel at the tuck in front, she walked and skipped back to her two friends.

I got to know them over summer's last days. Ashley played the loud friend. Not as shapely as the other two, she made up for her heavy legs and slight belly roll with obscenities—she cursed like a luckless fisherman. Jill was cock-sure cool. A sharp smile with the shape and eyes a boy—or a lifeguard—could get lost in. She had it all.

I stood there in the middle of the boardwalk, watching them. I felt shaky and made my way to that bench.

It took Linda as long to say goodbye to her friends as it took Romeo to say good night to Juliet. As she headed my way, untucking and tucking her towel, I took a deep breath. She plunked down next to me and gave me a kiss on the cheek. The wind blew her hair on and off her face and smile.

"Isn't it great!"

"Super-duper."

"What's the matter?"

"Nothing. I'm very relieved. Very happy. But."

She folded her arms and looked at the traffic. She pointed at the Caddy, "Uh-oh. You're getting a ticket on your windshield. What's your car's name?"

"You must be thinking of my other car. That's just the Caddy. And you know that's not the but."

"That's it—Caddy. That's not a name?"

"It's the kind of car."

"I don't know. How'm I supposed to know about fifty-year-old cars?"

"Do you remember my questions?"

"Nope. Okay. What was your tenth question after the three squared one?"

The time sitting on the bench before she came down to meet me—that's the time that saved me from preaching. Her running to him told me all I needed to know. Who the hell was I? Not her father. All I did was watch out for her. But as a friend, well, I had some dues coming there.

"Where have you been? I've been worried sick about you since you left. I looked from here to Kansas."

"Sorry," she sat back. Then she stood up, held the towel at one end, and snapped it out. Sand flecked the boardwalk. "I can't keep track. It's all a blur." She folded the towel once, twice, and sat down. One leg crossed under her, she looked up at me. "I'm sorry, Uncle Jimmy." She dropped her eyes. "I left your place and went to the drugstore, except they just closed. So I rode to Jill's—she lives on Sussex, right down from Robin. She has her license, and she drove me to Shop-Rite, and their drugstore stays open late." She sat up and looked at me as if she'd solved world hunger. "And that's that," her hands wiped together.

"You might as well call me Jimmy. So where were you yesterday?"

"At Jill's. We partied with her mom. She is so cool."

"Have you eaten today?"

She looked at her stomach and gathered tummy skin. "I don't need to eat with this."

"Don't give me that," I stood up. "C'mon. We'll load your bike up, and I'll take you to get something to eat."

"What about the Commodore? I thought you were supposed to go to the Commodore with Ronny?"

"Screw Ronny."

"But you were just together. You two were looking for me together."

"Is that what he told you?"

"Yes."

"What else did he tell you?"

"That Jill and Ashley and I can come to his beach anytime."

"Jill whose mom parties with her. What did you say?"

"I said sure. I didn't want to piss off Jill. She likes him. She's seventeen. I told you she has her license."

The diabolical son of a bitch. I shook my head to clear my thoughts.

"Listen to me. You're swinging too hard." Not being her father didn't stop my father from speaking up.

"What?"

"When a batter hits. You're swinging the bat too hard. It's a baseball metaphor. Remember metaphors? We talked about them. You're trying to hit a home run every time, and you can't. Nobody can."

"So it's like getting to first base, then second base and third. Like the Meat Loaf song."

"Sugar shit. No. Not like the Meat Loaf song. That's a different metaphor. You're trying too hard to please people who don't give a shit about you."

I watched the blue sky, the passing traffic, and one stark-white sea gull as it flew past. I imagined myself back in my parents' kitchen, looking at the clock as the old man wound down after a Friday night inquisition. I hate giving personal advice. It's like handing somebody the keys to a car with bald tires.

After a minute or so, Linda pipped up, "You were right. I am hungry. Why didn't you just say what you meant? Metaphors are stupid." She stood up, presented me with her towel, and took my hand. "Sugar shit. I like that. Let's go see what amazing leftovers you have in your fridge."

On the way to the Caddy, I pictured what I had. A kind SUV let me back out, and we pulled into traffic. The boardwalk looked full of colors now. Hints of sunshine off cars beamed brighter. Linda fiddled with the radio and found a song she liked—I didn't know it. She sang along in her whisper voice.

Who's that girl Who's that girl/ When you see her, say a prayer and kiss your heart goodbye/ She's trouble, in a word get closer to the fire.

We passed the Commodore. She turned and looked after it. "You're not going in?"

"I have an underage guest."

"You could say you were my Dad."

I laughed.

"I like it when you laugh. Almost as much as when you get mad. How's that song go? Squeeze play, it's gonna be close. Holy cow, I think he's gonna make it!"

I smiled for two blocks.

At home I stood in front of an open and damn fridge. Linda leaned in, hands clasped behind her back, staring. "I haven't seen Ronny since way back if that's what made you mad."

"Leaning over, you look like a short, big-haired umpire."

"That's a simile." She straightened up, eyes darting all around. "Seriously, I am seriously starving."

I spotted a possibility. "Go sit down. Here," I pulled a Pepsi from its plastic ring. "I'll have something in twenty minutes."

I put a pot of water on to boil and found the ziti. I had some frozen, sweet Italian sausages, and against my unwritten rule concerning meat, I defrosted them in the microwave and cut them up. Then I got an egg and the half-container of leftover ricotta. I beat the egg, added fresh-ground Parmigiano-Reggiano, and basil from my balcony herbs. I drained the ziti before it was done, spooned in the ricotta mixture, sausages, and—Aunt Nellie forgive me—something in a can called Pizza Quik that Alice bought me back when I got home from Florida. I let it bubble all together for about a minute before I spooned it into a Pyrex dish—a little more ground cheese on top, thank you—and popped it right into the oven for twenty minutes.

I heard, "Twenty minutes," and looked out at my impatient guest.

"It's been ten."

"Closer to fifteen."

I pulled two Pabst from the fridge, pooped them both and handed one to Linda. She had MTV videos on. "Sip this, be happy, and turn that music down."

"A beer? Cool, thanks! Why don't you like new music? You play old, dead, black people."

"They can't be old and dead at once." I headed for the balcony. "Like you said, twenty minutes. My timer's set." I slid the door closed, sat down, and fired up a big cigar I had bought in the event of celebration or disaster. I smoked it like a cigarette down to its middle, and then doused it with a pour of Pabst.

Air, beautifully clear, cool air blew off the ocean. I could have salted the ziti's water with that air. Damn the town was full. I hummed "Going to a Go-Go" in the time it took a blue pick-up to travel two blocks on Ocean Ave.

August tourists can be desperate, near death, or part of what I call a gathered outing. Young people fill the first category. Desperate because time's short. If they'd stuck with the same partner all summer, the decision deadline floated just over the next wave. If their summer had been empty, if they'd played the third wheel, Labor Day would claim most of the good prospects.

White-haired, near-death people show up on buses. Dressed in white slacks or seersucker, they stay at inland hotels, eat free breakfasts, and play pinochle around a pool. At night, the house-hired male dancer grabs ladies away from their grasshopper or brandy alexander and pulls them out under a temporary glow ball. The seated women clap and smile. The husbands stare. Families form the gathered outing. With school just around the fireplug, pop gathers up as many paying members of the extended family as possible and rents a house for a week or two. Grandparents get to see grandchildren, mothers get to share a kitchen and childcare, and the husbands sit on the beach staring at the desperate girls.

That cigar had me going. It had me restless again. I started to think about Linda's comment about my taste in music. I had some newer records—I just hadn't played them because they didn't mean summer to me. I had one somebody had brought over and left years ago—Warren Zevon recorded live at the Roxy—I thought she might like. "Werewolves of London"—she'd know that song.

I went inside. I got greeted with the requisite glance followed by the look-away, so I felt no guilt when I muted MTV. I found the Zevon album and turned it way up. The record was in good shape. I went to town.

I bounced around to the beginning, and then took these big, menacing werewolf steps in time to the music. When the chorus came on—*Rahooo! Werewolves of London!*—I put my head back like I was howling. I didn't know the whole song—just the chorus and end.

Linda beamed watching me. She swiveled around on the sofa, her legs underneath her. I only saw her smile. I didn't give a shit about her yellow bathing suit or her sand-flecked feet on my furniture. She wasn't pregnant. That's all I knew. She smiled at my silly act. I tried not to hack my head off from all my prancing.

I finished great—got the lyrics right and combed both hands through my temples when Zevon sang ...*and his hair was perfeeect!* After it finished, I stood there puffing.

"Was that a live white man?" Linda smiled.

I had to sit. I caught my breath for a minute and looked at her. "Barely, in my case."

She swiveled back toward the TV. Up went the volume. I watched a video to its finish. "Don't you see the video every time you hear the song?"

"What?" She didn't look away from the set.

"I mean, don't you imagine the video? See it in your head when you hear the song?"

I thought it was an innocent question. For some reason she slumped down on the couch as if she'd been shot.

"Sometimes."

I got up, walked to the kitchen, and checked my timer. "Four minutes. We're not quite ready to go under the broiler.

"What?"

"Not quite ready. The ziti has a few—"

"Fuck the ziti!" She came off the couch, steered straight for the bathroom, and slammed the door.

I walked over and knocked. "Linda?"

Nothing.

"Linda? What the heck's going on?"

I turned down the TV volume, and in the quiet I heard her sobbing. I turned off the TV and came back. I tried the knob—it was locked.

"Linda? I have to put the...I'll be right back."

I turned off the oven. Back again, I put my ear to the bathroom door. The sobbing had turned into a high pitched, steady whine. I had no idea what the hell to do. I got about half pissed off. First my shitty day at Loch Arbour taking crap from the borstal boys, then the ride with Mr. Wristlock, and now my ziti overcooking. Not to mention that damn appointment tomorrow morning.

I taped the door with a knuckle. "What's going on? You should be celebrating."

"Oh, just give me a minute."

I gave her ten. Closer to twelve. I know because I watched the clock just to feed my frustration.

Then I thought the hell with it, turned on the broiler, and stood there, leaning over every few seconds to watch the top of the ziti bubble golden brown. I opened the oven door all the way, pulled out the rack, potholders in both hands.

Just as it came off the rack, the casserole dish slipped. I moved my hands to catch it, and the underside of my right wrist—the same one Ronny wrenched—pressed against the oven rack. I jerked back with pain. I caught the casserole of bubbling ziti with my left potholder—one end of the casserole. It tilted, flipped over, and spilled out ziti all over the oven door. Steam and smoke curled up from the oozing mess. It spread over the window well like lava. I used both potholders to lift the dish, but I couldn't grip it. I managed to grab the son of a bitch before the heat from the oven melted my face. At the sink, I put down the casserole and hit the cold water to let it run over my wrist. Cold water splashed the casserole. Yes, Pyrex can fail.

A few minutes under the water did my wrist good. I loaded my pipe. A few tokes on it settled my nerves. The bathroom door opened, and I heard a sniff-sniff behind me.

She sat on the couch across from me. In the excitement, I hadn't heard the shower come on. Her hair dripped as she cocked her head to one side and rubbed the other dry. She had my big Yankee beach towel with the top hat and bat logo wrapped around her. She looked like a kid again without that yellow suit.

"Hope you like ziti a la oven door," I waved a hand at the kitchen.

She stood up and looked. "Why's the oven open?" One hand went up to her mouth, the other held on tight to the towel's knot on her chest. "Oh, my," she walked closer.

"I could spread some cheese on top and get a couple of big spoons. We could pretend we're camping."

"I'll clean it up."

"Go get dressed."

"It's my fault."

"Sure. The ziti heard you, felt bad, and jumped to its death."

She bent over. "Do you have a sponge or something? To wipe it with?"

"Don't worry about it. We're going out to eat."

"I can push it all onto a plate or something."

I opened the silverware drawer and got two forks. I handed one to Linda. Then I took a taste. I saw a sausage chunk and speared it.

"What are you doing?"

"Somebody once told me good cooks always taste as they cook. Go get dressed."

Linda started laughing. She plowed her fork into the pile and tasted. "Umm. Forgive me, ziti. You are truly tasty." She dropped her fork in the sink and saw the spilt casserole. "Oh. Sorry about that."

I shooed her out of the kitchen. "Go. Mebbe's Famous awaits."

"What?"

"Mebbe's Famous. That's where we're going."

She had spare clothes in Ronny's old room. One Tuesday night, she left a knapsack full of shorts and shirts. She had her make-up, lip balms, and one or two pairs of flip-flops in there, too. Every Tuesday night, she forgot something when she left after our lesson. I kept putting things in the room. Ronny's things were long gone.

In the bathroom, the hairdryer came on. That I bought her. I never used one. I figured the mess would be there when I got back. I planned on dropping Linda off at home. Before the hairdryer quit, I phoned Peggy.

"I'm dropping Linda off in an hour or so."

"Where the hell was she?"

"I saw her sitting on a bench on the boardwalk."

"I don't know what to say. I'm sure as hell glad she turned up."

"She's just fine. You know she's safe with an old, gay man."

"Oh, go on."

I waited for her to say, you're not old. No luck, though. "About an hour," and I hung up.

Linda came out of the bathroom ready to go. Scrubbed. That's the word that came to mind when I saw her. Maybe it's a male thing, or a father thing. The way she smiled before she spoke filled my heart.

"What's a Mebbe's?"

"Mebbe's, my dear, is fried sea food. You mean to tell me you don't know about Mebbe's?"

"Where is it?"

"Right here in town."

"Oh, and I'm sorry. I mean about all my fuss."

I opened the door to the stairs. "What fuss?"

"My bathroom tantrum."

I locked up. I did not want any visitors waiting for me when I returned. "All is forgotten."

We headed down the stairs. She bounced from one cloud to the next. "Margaret always asks what the hell's the matter with me. What the hell's all this goddamn crying about? That's what she yells."

I didn't know. I could guess. Guessers should just move on.

9

W E STOOD IN Mebbe's looking up at the big menu sign on the wall behind the counter.

"The fare combines simplicity with economy. You can pay twenty bucks for a shrimp dinner across the street at Dave's. Here a platter's $4.50."

"It says Fried everywhere."

Mebbe's served clams, scallops, shrimp, and flounder—all fried and served as a sandwich or platter with French fries, tarter or cocktail sauce included.

"A platter comes with fries and coleslaw."

"Hot dogs and hamburgers for the landlubber," Linda read.

"Oh, and of course, we could get a bucket of steamers."

"For a beverage, grape, orange, or fruit punch belly slosh."

"Or a Coke."

Linda decided on a fried shrimp platter. I ordered the same, along with a small bucket of steamers. Ordering the bucket made me remember Ronny teaching Robin how to eat steamers on their first dinner date.

Mrs. Mebbe took our orders. Dressed in one of her torn, spattered moo-moos, her heavy, bra-less breasts swayed as she turned, cupped a hand, and yelled our orders back to Murray, her son, who prepared everything while Mom handled the register.

"To go or stay?" She turned to us.

"We'll eat next door."

I took Linda's arm and showed her where to go. "You wait here." Next door were four picnic tables. It was the original Mebbe's before they expanded into the bigger building right alongside. No table service—just a spot to camp and eat.

When everything came up, I carried it all over to Linda.

55

I couldn't remember the last time I had to give a how-to-eat steamer lesson, let alone to a 15-year-old hormone hurricane. Thankfully she'd never seen an uncircumcised male. Judging from her comments just a guess.

"Watch and learn." I grabbed the neck's skin between my forefinger and thumb and peeled it off. Linda's eyes got wider. "Then a little dip and wash in the clam broth, followed by a butter bath." I wiped the butter from my chin and spread my hands. I pointed at her, handed her a nice one. "Now you."

"Is this its wiener?"

"Some call it the foot, some call it the neck."

"Man, that would be some wiener on a guy, like if a guy had half his length down there. Half this steamer's this thing. And I take this dark skin off?"

"Like taking off a sock. Watch again." I put my voice down—it doesn't get along with melted butter. It was strictly show with no tell for the rest of the meal.

"So I peel it."

I shook my head.

"Give it a bath. Is that to wash off sand?"

Another nod.

"And into the butter." She put it in her mouth and looked at me as if I'd betrayed her deepest secret. A hesitant, "Mmm" was followed by a smile. I watched her jaw—nothing. She just tasted butter. She hadn't chewed the clam.

I tapped the table, looked at her, and gnashed my teeth together like a set of fake TV choppers.

"Okay," she mumbled. She lifted another clam into her mouth, moved her jaw around, and swallowed. "There."

After two more, she bit into a sandy stomach, turned, and spit everything into a napkin.

I got a butter high finishing off the rest of the bucket. Between inhaling ketchup with some French fries, Linda took apart her fried shrimp sandwich.

I looked at her, parted my hands and shrugged.

"Checking for tails." She lifted each shrimp from its bun-resting place, examined it as if she was an archeologist examining a fossil, and then tucked it back in its spot.

As she sized up another shrimp, I wiped my hands clean and picked up my voice. "You may as well be from Nebraska."

She looked at me and let the shrimp drop.

"Do you want a hot dog?"

"Do they deep fry those, too?"

"They do. Then a nice sizzle on the grill. Too bad you weren't around in the old days. This right here, where we're sitting," I waved a hand, "was the whole place. No tables, no place to sit and eat. You got a platter between two paper plates, and sometimes Mrs. Mebbe grabbed a handful of warm fries fresh out of the grease and tossed them in your brown bag as a bonus."

"Charming. After handling the money."

"Next door where we got the food was an auto parts place, and on the corner sat a Sinclair gas station with the green dinosaur sign."

"Why'd they have a dinosaur on their sign?"

"That's where oil comes from. Fossil fuel?"

She stared at me the same way as when she put the first steamer in her mouth.

"We used to joke that Mebbe's sold their old oil to the Sinclair station. That it was so thick and old, it could pass for 10w30."

"I don't know what that is. This is a rip-off," she picked up the coleslaw. It came served in a tiny paper bucket, maybe two heaping tablespoons.

"Yeah, that's not a big deal."

She took the top half of her hamburger bun—at Mebbe's everything comes on a hamburger bun except a hot dog—and wiped her paper plate clean of ketchup. The child loved carbohydrates.

"You want my French fries?" I pushed my plate toward her.

"Thank you."She gave her plate with the dissected shrimp sandwich a backhand away and went to town on my fries. She plunked one into her mouth, turned to the traffic on F Street and said, "So you're not mad at me?"

"For what?"

"Ronny."

"We've been through this."

"It all came back the last few days."

"That kind of thing has a way of doing that."

"What kind of thing?"

"Adult things. Things that can be final."

"Antony's final."

I wiped my hands and took hers. "Sometimes regret comes back. I know, believe me. It's nothing to be ashamed of. You're a better person for remembering him and keeping him in your thoughts."

"It's guilt. That's what Margaret told me. I'm feeling guilty."

"I don't go to that school anymore."

"What?"

"Guilt, my ass. Guilty about what?"

"About Antony and Ronny. What happened with Ronny."

"Look, I don't know what exactly had you upset before. If it's Ronny, treat him like that sandy clam you got. Spit him out. Forget about him," I held up my free arm, "and eat the damn fries."

She put both hands in her lap, tilted her head back and laughed. Then her elbows lifted, smacked down on the table, and she leaned forward. "Fuck that clam," she smiled, raising a palm.

"There you go," I smiled back and gave her five.

We cleaned up our mess—Mrs. Mebbe never came from behind the counter to show off that moo-moo—and I drove Linda home.

"Don't go anywhere until your mother sees you. I don't want her visiting me on Friday and giving me hell."

She opened the door but held the handle. "Tomorrow's Thursday."

"I'm off tomorrow, remember?"

"That's tomorrow? Your doctor's appointment?"

"Yup. Fun stuff."

"You want me to go with you? I can get Jill to come with us."

"Jill whose mother drinks with her."

"Yuppers."

"That's okay. I'll be back in the afternoon. It won't—oh, what the hell. Go see your mother."

She put a foot on the street, stopped, and slid back across the seat. She planted one on my cheek. Scooting back, she said, "Thanks for dinner!" and slammed the door behind her. I watched her into the house, drove down to Ocean Ave, and stopped. South to the Commodore, north to home.

It was a simple decision. One way or the other. Loneliness and a congealed, cheesy mess one-way, familiar faces spouting abuse the other. I headed south.

As I made the turn, I wished I had a cigarette, because Cousin Brucie on101.1 picked that moment to spin the Four Tops' "Sugar Pie Honey Bunch." I told myself summer made the decision for me. Fresh from Mebbe's, it had steered me south toward the Commodore.

Like a religious man spared from disaster, hearing that song told me I'd picked the right direction, but a second after I cranked the volume, a rip of thunder overhead damn near jumped me through the Caddy's top. People who look to everyday events as signs or karma crack me up.

I turned north to celebrate—no mini-Ronny—and gloat to his face. I passed the hotel—the Engine Room hummed at 6,500 RPM. There was a band playing—more neighborhood atmosphere for the locals living on Monmouth. The owners didn't have much time to make up for the fire's loss of revenue.

Then it hit me. Between my appointment tomorrow and all the excitement with Linda, I'd forgotten all about me getting banned from the Commodore courtesy of my glass throwing. I had a court date in a few weeks. What a dumb ass. Driving home, I shook my head, laughing.

See what I mean about signs?

10

THE NEXT DAY, after my visit with Dr. Doom and associates, I stood eyeing a fruity concoction's ad on the lunch special chalkboard—Try our new Rum-Belly's Vengeance (Limit two per customer)—at Evelyn's Tiki Bar & Restaurant. The place overlooked the Shrewsbury River where Ocean Ave runs on a thin sliver of land between the river and ocean from above Monmouth Beach to Sea Bright. On my back, I felt the noon sun push aside the last of the morning cool.

A hostess came over. "Eating indoors or staying out today?

"Out, please."

"One?"

"I'll sit at the bar, thanks." Then I saw it. I wasn't going to sit at a bar with grass skirts hung from its edge and decorated with sappy, smiley-face coconuts. "On second thought, I'll take a table."

I could see calm river and smell ocean—it may have been the river at low tide. Except for two older couples who were dressed like they were in some posh club—white slacks and sport coats on the gents, dresses on the ladies—I had the place to myself.

My mind went blank. Given the news I'd just received, I waited for a moment of clarity—some great epiphany or sudden realization of wisdom. Hell, I couldn't recall one quarter of a tit of what the doctor told me. No giant list fell, uncurling as it dropped, of things I wanted or had to do. I didn't retain one piece of scheduled business which required immediate attention. It's on the printout, I told myself.

The one immediate memory that stuck in my head was my father. I'd watched him wither to skin and bones, and for decades afterward in all my dreams, he remained the thin shell of a man he'd become near the end. There was no way in hell I was putting Alice through that.

"I'll try one of those," I pointed to the chalkboard when a young girl with a bright smile came to my table. She didn't blink at my EL.

I sat there and fiddled with my knife, flicking it back and forth from finger to finger, wondering what possessed me to order a sickly-sweet, rum-bomb of a cocktail. Maybe because the doctor—believe it or not, I forget his name—gave me so many options. A Chinese menu with five folds.

"My doctor recommended this drink," I told the waitress when she lowered it down to me. "I must experience what a two-drink max drink does for me."

"Who's your doctor?"

A waitress who murdered levity. She smiled the way a girl standing with her back against plywood and balloons next to her ears smiled at the knife thrower.

"After two of these monsters, can I have a beer with my burger?"

"Oh, sure," she shook her head. "I think so. Why not? Let me go check."

She skipped back with the news.

"I checked. Manager says a beer with your burger's just fine."

I watched the bartender fix it. Dark rum, light rum, vodka, pineapple juice, lime juice, grenadine, simple syrup, and a float of 151 rum. Even the fruit garnish got a soaking—two maraschino cherries between half a pineapple slice stuck together with a swizzle sword. A yellow paper umbrella and blue plastic straw finished everything off.

I sucked it right down. It came close to one of my 50-50 drivers in my 16-ounce Burger King Yankee cup. No big deal. The garnish drizzled with 151 was the highlight.

I received number two.

"This is your second rum-belly," the waitress reminded me.

"Rum-Belly's capitalized on your chalkboard. Was Rum-Belly a pirate?"

She frazzled her mouth. "I never got asked that before. I don't know."

"Blackbeard's a famous pirate. I wouldn't want a drink named any color beard."

Her mouth untwisted into a smile—this time, though, the smile reminded me of the ones on the coconuts. "I know about him," she huffed.

"Since you ask, I imagine the drink's named that to maintain our pirate, tiki, and Caribbean themes." She spun around on a beer cap and hurried off.

I almost reached for her. I didn't mean it, I wanted to call. I'm sorry I'm being a smart ass, but you see I'm just now coming from the oncologist.

It didn't matter. In that moment of watching her turn to leave just as I wanted to speak to her, to anyone, I realized what I would do after Labor Day. I imagined an overcast of clouds parting and seeing Ireland from the plane, my breath escaping me as if my lungs have been pierced with thousands of tiny pins. Cape-shaped farms of green, darkening then growing brighter, then a whole other shade sweeping down from a hilltop.

I never ordered that beer and burger. I had places to go. I left a ten buck tip. By the time I got to the Caddy, I had myself in cruise control.

Drop top down—check. Radio blaring, cigarette burning. I knew how to do this. Slow's the word. Twenty-five, baby. Twenty-five, no more, no less, all the way down Ocean Ave. Even passing through Deal where the limit shot up, I kept the speed down. Ideas that swirled in my head would have to wait. I put on the invisible driving blinders, watched the crosswalks, and hoped nobody on a bike rammed me. Limit of two Rum-Belly's Vengeance per customer.

Hearing my tires spin over the Inlet Bridge steel grating sounded like home. At the bridge's apex, the town welcomed me back. Ocean Ave widened before intersecting Inlet Ave, the bright flower beds of Inlet's island park along with kids and bikes crossing the park's paths—they all greeted me. The sun aligned with Ocean Ave. If I could have seen all the way to the end of town, the big brick gate halves that bordered Spring Lake might have served as Sarsen stones on the solstice. I even winked at the dance bar as I drove past. Kelway Enterprises my ass.

I knew where I was going. I took the long way, the scenic route. I drove all the way to those Spring Lake gates—maybe Belmar built them, I don't know—turned around and headed back north. I lit a smoke and played the radio nice and loud. Alms to summer in return for her memories. From June's solstice till that day in late August, I'd lived like summer. Day to day, hour to hour, top down.

It is the easiest thing in the world to forget that we are free agents, that we can reason or will our way back from the brink of a self-made precipice, that words and deeds do matter.

One day at the beach as a boy of eight I had me a brand-new beach ball. My father bought it for me as a reward for building the second-place car in the Pinewood Derby. All I had to do was blow it up. I asked my father if he would help.

He watched me take it from its plastic wrapping. "Pretty windy today, James. Might want to save that for the yard."

I insisted in my quiet way.

He smiled and told me, "Okay, but you blow it up yourself. Then you'll know who to blame if it sets sail for France."

It took me quite a while to get the thing nearly round, and the old man, of course, was right. Blow it did after a few punches and kicks. It was high tide, and atop the water, it rode backwash out, came in on the shore break—just out of my reach—then retreated again. I figured it would wash back in again, but no—a breeze lifted it just before the next wave, and it settled on the surface past the break line. Seconds later, it was past the first barrel—way over my head at high tide.

The old man, asleep with a towel over his face, the guards, Teresa, and the Marys—nobody noticed. On the strength of a fine, crisp, offshore breeze, it bobbed further and further away, colors spinning, growing smaller until the glare off the surface and my tears turned me west.

I could have snagged the son of a bitch if I'd had the balls to dive in after that first wave.

I came to 514 Barclay Ave, the home of Thomas and Rosemary Silva. Typical Belmar neighborhood. Houses smushed together; a flag or two out front; a front porch three or four steps up; concrete sidewalks poured decades ago lifted crooked by tree roots; the grass strip bordering the curb manicured with petunias circling an old sycamore; the next strip treeless.

I had not met Thomas Silva. I'd met Rosemary, his wife, when I'd told her about her son's phone call, his destination, and the reason behind it. I slowed almost to a stop, checking in my mirror for oncoming traffic. The house, which reminded me of Robin's, looked empty. No car in the driveway, all the shades pulled down. No trash cans out on trash day, no paper waiting on the front walk. The porch furniture I sat on with Mrs. Silva had been removed, perhaps put away for the summer. The Caddy pulled itself over directly in front of the house.

On the other side of the street a few houses down, a car sat parked in the driveway of 519 Barclay Ave, the home of Mrs. Gloria Gilbert. I did not know if a Mr. Gilbert resided there as well, but I guessed as much because in the letter I wrote for Linda, I imagined Antony had told me the Mustang had been a gift from Mrs. Gilbert's old man. Would a middle-aged boyfriend woo a woman of Mrs. Gilbert's likeness—I saw her interviewed on the local news—with a car? Of course, the term old man had been of my own choosing. I doubted Antony would have used such an anachronistic expression even if he'd known the car's origin from the story in the *Press*.

Across the street from Mrs. Gilbert lived Mrs. Mary Stevens. It was she who had heard Mrs. Gilbert's screams, had seen the white Mustang race down Barclay, and had later heard, along with the entire town, the first aid siren. Her testimony may have become vital to the police in the identification of the alleged suspect—the *Press*, in that day's late edition, also used the word perpetrator. Unfortunately, she failed to see the driver. Mrs. Silva knew her son had made a phone call before becoming agitated. She had heard Antony swear loudly and slam the front door on his way out.

When the siren sounded, she must have wondered, perhaps dreaded. The way only a mother can. Now I wondered. Had my visit weeks ago brought any relief to her and her husband, or had contemplation of meaningless events and coincidences leading up to Antony's death caused them more pain? Had they moved in with relatives? Unable or unwilling to drive Belmar's streets, to pass the Gilbert house, to venture uptown where the crane's top at Sterner's Lumber loomed high above F Street roofs, had they deserted their home? From reports, they had to know Antony's route by heart.

I pulled out. I knew Antony's last trip. Somewhere along E Street, Antony spotted the police. Maybe they saw him first. Nine stop signs. Most of them run, I didn't know exactly how many. The police report stated several stop signs were ignored. I stopped at each. No police car rode on my tail, cherry top flashing and siren screaming.

Locust Ave widens at its eastern end where it merges with North Lake Drive. From there it's four blocks, four more stop signs, before B Street ends at Terrace Road, where the homes of Inlet Terrace surround the lagoon. Heading north leaving B Street, a car has three options: make a quick right onto Brystol, bear left on Terrace Road which follows Inlet Terrace and dead-ends, or bear right and continue to Inlet Ave. The road bends ninety degrees onto Inlet Ave. Go straight ahead through the curve, and you'll ram through

Will Kelly's hedge and across his watered lawn until Shark River Inlet stops you.

Antony flew through all four stop signs. His car careened left, over corrected, then continued straight. As I bore right after the last stop sign, I noticed that the start of Will Kelly's driveway aligned with the left lane of Terrace Road. Following my lane through the curve would take me through Kelly's hedge. The damage had been repaired—five newly planted privets stood gap-toothed between mature growths. Antony didn't try for the driveway. He kept going straight. No brake marks either on the road or across Kelly's yard could be detected by police. The Mustang struck the lip of the Inlet bulkhead at a high rate of speed.

Nobody was behind me. I slowed to a stop and pulled over along Terrace Road just before the curve onto Inlet alongside a No Parking Anytime sign. I waited for a car coming down Inlet to round the curve. Then I pulled across the road and trespassed onto Kelly's driveway. It curved to the left toward the house—a large, lavish structure, its eaves decorated with trellis and detailed trim, it sat atop a rise that began at the river bulkhead like some ancient battlement guarding a waterway.

I let the Caddy coast to the bulkhead, stopped the engine, and climbed out. Early afternoon—I figured Will sat in one of his establishments going over the books. I didn't know if a Mrs. Will existed, let alone if she was at home.

Maybe twenty feet to the right of the Caddy, I found the marks I wanted to see on the bulkhead. The lip rose six or so inches from the ground. A row of white gravel stone stretched three feet out from the bulkhead along the vast, green lawn.

I sat next to one of the scars. A diagonal gash three inches deep splintered the bulkhead lip before shrinking to barely a scratch. New white wood stretched atop the lip. Out over the water, gulls circled something. They waited, heads down, wings bending.

I looked back at the house. Seeing the property from the rear, I realized the lot was pear shaped with the stem located out front where Terrace Road split left and right. The wide, flat bottom followed the Inlet's bulkhead.

I looked down into the water—a foot, foot and a half rolling swells. Seaweed clung to a straight line on the bulkhead four feet above the swirls— tide coming in. Will Kelly's dock, a platform with circle clamps riding two fat pipes anchored to the bulkhead, screamed metal-on-metal as it rose and fell with the wake. A big Boston Whaler passed, its twin black 100 hp Mercs opened wide, throaty. The driver and his female passenger leaned forward and pitched back as the Whaler smacked crest then plowed into trough again and again. The boat kept going toward the Inlet Bridge, maybe headed out to sea and on to New York. Seeing New York from the harbor is seeing New York for the first time.

The boat rode closer to the south side on the far right of the channel, and I marked when it passed over the spot, the black mud spot that poured from inside and around the white Mustang as the crane's stretched cable vibrated, a giant harp string splashing water gobs big as coffee mugs.

All those mordant bastards standing along the bulkhead from B Street past A Street. Wonder if the car's paid for? Who'll cash in on insurance? Hope he likes sea food. Trying to catch a glimpse, leaning this way and that to see a lifeless boy's body flopping inside a dangling, stolen car.

I know because I stood with them. My view from where I sat on Kelly's bulkhead—that perspective drew me closer. I could feel the water's rush as the waves swelled and swished up against the bulkhead up and down the inlet. This was ocean water in a funnel. As the inlet widened closer to Shark River, it calmed. Not here, not in the funnel's stem.

Behind me, a man's voice called. I swiveled around on the bulkhead's lip to look. Some guy—it wasn't Will Kelly—stood at the bottom of Will Kelly's back steps, waving his arms at me as if I was a ship he'd sighted after being marooned for twenty years.

He yelled himself a hernia. For a second, I thought I'd had a stroke. I didn't understand a word. Then I realized English was not this guy's mother tongue. He had dark, curly hair, a slim build, and wore a white button-down shirt, black slacks, and black bow tie.

I smiled at him, stood up, and showed my palms to the sky. He made Xs with his hands in front of his face. He pointed at the Caddy, jabbed a finger at it.

"For chrissakes," I mouthed.

I walked over to the Caddy, got the summons from Kelway Enterprises out of the glove compartment, and started up the yard toward the house. I held the summons up in front of me and grinned at the son of a bitch as if I'd just thrown down a straight flush. He came a few steps to meet me. He'd stopped flailing.

We met closer to the house than the bulkhead. Puffing a little—that yard was steep—I pointed to the summons. "Mr. Kelly—"

"Mr. Kelly. Out, out."

"Hey, you speak English."

"Mr. Kelly. Out! Out!"

He leaned toward me. Then he took several quick steps. We stood face to face. And then his eyes fell to my stoma. I've seen it enough to know. He made an O with his mouth and covered it with a hand. He dropped that hand and found the other at his waist. Brow furrowed, he clucked his tongue. We stood there and looked at each other.

"This," I touched near my stoma. "No voice. This is my voice." I held up my EL.

He stared at me for a second and then bowed his head.

I held out the summons to him. "It's okay. Don't worry about it. Give this to Mr. Kelly," I smiled. I shook it for him to take it.

"Mr. Kelly." He took the summons, glanced at it, and then dropped his hands to his sides. He stood at attention. "Thank you."

"You are welcome."

A slight smile started to grow on his face.

I gestured a hand, "Tell Mr. Kelly to shove that up his ass."

His smile exploded—whiter-than-white teeth—and he shook all over like a winner on The Price Is Right. "Up your ass! Douchebag! Illiterate spot-headed son of a bitch!"

I bent over, hysterical, went to one knee, and brought up enough phlegm to lubricate a tank tread.

"Mr. Kelly says that?" I gasped between hacks.

He put a hand on my shoulder. "Yes, Mr. Kelly."

After a minute, I finished up and stood straight. "My name's Jimmy Hanlon," I held out a hand.

"Jimmy Hanlon. I am Rizvan." A gentle grip held my hand longer than the usual shake time.

"Goodbye, Rizvan." I tried to roll the invisible "h" like he did.

He held the summons behind his butt and made a few quick motions. "Shove up your ass!"

"Will Kelly's ass."

"Yes! Will Kelly's ass!"

In the Caddy I waved at him as he watched me pull out. I thought about revving that 429, spinning her tires, and shooting some gravel onto Kelly's lawn, but I figured Rizvan might have to pick it up. I pictured him kneeling with a pail, plinking gravel into it one stone at a time.

Home felt nice and cool. I'd cleaned it up the night before. Either way, I didn't want the hassle of straightening out little things after hearing from the doctor.

I made myself a screwdriver in my Burger King Yankee cup and took it out on the balcony. One hell of a lot of people on the beach for a Thursday. Tomorrow, the last Friday before Labor Day weekend, I'd be close to home. I'd spend some time with The Lipp before I went on the clock; I'd have a nice, relaxing morning.

Watching two kids—boys, about thirteen, I guessed—cross Ocean Ave from the boards to Mercer, I thought about Ronny. Then I thought about Ronny and Robin. They were in the home stretch. The last week of summer, graduation night, the steady beau boarding the bus for boot camp.

I thought about Alice and the girls when I watched a family unload the minivan after parking in Will Kelly's lot. A little girl, maybe three, wrapped a pink, blow-up seahorse around her waist and jumped up and down holding onto it. Dad came around from the driver's side, said something to Mom, and the inflatable went back in the van. World War II caused fewer tears. The kid cried away as the rest of the crew got stuff from the van. She'd run out of breath, stop, suck in air, and wail it back out. When her parents and siblings—three of them, all older than her—stood ready, she wouldn't go. Finally, big brother hoisted her up. She pointed back at the car the whole way across the lot.

Clouds parted, and sunlight moved across the lot as if from behind an opening door. The green flag on the Mercer Ave guard stand blew straight west in the onshore breeze. Glare sparkled off the water and formed tiny suns on windshields passing along Ocean Ave. All that light bright in my eyes. I had to close them.

Inside I put my usual stack of favorites on: Smokey Robinson and the Miracles Greatest Hits Vol. 2, the original Broadway cast soundtrack of *South Pacific* with Mary Martin and Ezio Pinza, and The Four Tops Greatest Hits.

Those drums and familiar old scratches on "Going to a Go-Go" sounded better than ever. I decided to make myself chicken cacciatore.

In the middle of defrosting, cutting, slicing, browning, and every other prep required for a palatable chicken cacciatore—I remember Mary Martin belted out being as corny as Kansas in August—I decided I'd go to the library after dinner.

I found my favorite book about Ireland, *Ancient Irish Sites*, and read about Dun Aengus, the Burren, and Newgrange. I also looked up the name of the man who had made my day—Rizvan. Names have meanings that go way back. Mrs. Toner helped me find the correct book. Rizvan means harbinger of good news.

I spent the evening on my balcony. I didn't have anything else to drink, and I stayed away from the weed. I had work the next day, and I'd had my fill of thinking. I didn't phone anybody. Linda and Robin were the only two people who knew about my appointment unless Robin told Ronny. I could deal with both. I wasn't worried about anyone finding out. They had their own concerns.

Summer nears Labor Day, and everybody drives in the fast lane heading downhill, cops be damned.

11

TIDES—THAT THOUGHT woke me up Friday, my first morning after my oncologist bummer. The mysteries of nature—I felt like an empty cup waiting to be filled with the day's events. The tide popped into my head.

I looked it up in my tide almanac—high tide this morning at 8:34 a.m. Across the globe on the opposite side of our Moon-stretched egg, it would be high tide at 8:34 a.m., and at the half-way point, low tide. My father used to tell us kids at low tide that all the water went across the ocean to visit Ireland. I think he had me in mind for the story. Teresa didn't fall for it. Neither did Mary Ellen—she never disagreed with Teresa—and Mary Jean hadn't come along yet.

I always followed the tide. Low tide meant good waves. High tide brought in shore break for most spots. I got a kick out of visitors to the shore who didn't know a thing about the oceans. They would ask the guards, "Is the tide coming in or going out?" The answer is yes. Always.

At my gates, I smiled and pointed to the chalkboard. There's a chalkboard at every gate with Forecast (always partly sunny, never partly cloudy), Water Temp (at least warmer by five degrees), Wind, and High Tide. Since I worked the early shift today, I'd write 8:34 on the High Tide blank, and then nod dozens of times when people asked, "So it's going out after 8:34?"

Since I felt wide awake, I fixed a coffee and Kahlua and headed down to the sand. The beach rake boys had run the shell-sweeping beast, and I plopped down right in the middle of their rake lines, soft as a snowdrift.

As the sun rose over the ocean, sky and water had their early debate over best dressed. The sky grew orange and pink-lit, one lone cloud hovering, shaped like a distant Long Island. The ocean edged along the Mercer Ave jetty with barely a whoosh, and at first light, threw a cobalt haze.

I didn't get a chance to vote. I stretched out on my blanket and caught a cat nap.

By seven, J's opened. The Lipp looked happy to have an early customer. I even sat at the counter to be social instead of heading outside. He poured me a coffee and offered to fill my thermos.

"It's full, but thanks."

"What the hell was I thinking?" he laughed. "Seamus, I got two weekends to make up a shitty July. Otherwise, winter's going to be cheap whiskey."

"Good forecast from Bryant Gumbel?"

"I don't watch that bastard. That Pauley woman's good looking, though." Lipp gave me a wink. "I stick to Good Morning America. I like that Marvin Hamlisch theme song."

"A fellow keyboard man."

"Yeah. Cream?"

"Please."

"It's milk." He pushed a *Press* to me across the counter. "Yesterday's news. Want it?"

"No thanks."

I got a hard roll with butter, took that and my thermos across Ocean Ave to a bench, and sat down. After a minute, I wished I'd taken that *Press*. Light glared at me off the empty water and across the sand, deserted in the morning cool. Behind me a few walkers passed, their voices blowing loud and soft, fading in the breeze.

I walked over to Annie's gate, dropped my stuff, and walked onto the sand to unlock the storage bin. I got Annie's chair and umbrella out for her. I set her umbrella up nice and secure by lashing the middle to the storm fence— something she never did. When I relieved her later, I could undo it for her. Her hands are a little arthritic—that's why she keeps them moving with the cross-stitch.

I meandered south. My first gate, Locust at ten o'clock, sat four blocks away. I kept an eye out for the Dog Lady. I figured I missed her, or she'd killed off her mutt from June and replaced it with a new victim, in which case she'd wait to break it in during the hottest part of the afternoon. I promised myself if I saw her with a different pooch, I'd report her ass to the SPCA.

In the hours after sunrise, the wind had shifted and turned counterclockwise. That meant a northeast push of wind and waves all day. Small splashy white caps began to lift in the day's full light. Waves broke in gentle leans to the south. I walked past my building and noticed my upstairs neighbor out on his balcony.

I daydreamed my way a few more blocks to the Lake Pavilion where I sat near my favorite gate—the one around back of the pavilion where the view is like my mural at home—and fired up one of the bones I'd rolled before the sunrise. Some people like to get a buzz on for the sunrise. I always considered it impressive enough.

A few weeks back, on a Saturday you couldn't step from boardwalk to ocean without trampling on the corner of a blanket, a woman coming up the ramp handed me a pair of ladies' sunglasses.

"I found them. Down there," she waved a hand at the ocean, "they washed right up at my feet in all those bubbles."

"Thank you," I took them. "I recognize these." A gorgeous, garish pair— the kind you'd see on a woman in a 60's spy movie—babushka and dark trench coat required.

"Really? That's amazing," she smiled.

Expensive with wide, tall, Polarized lens, they worked for me. The fact they flared up to a teardrop finish with silver colored inlay along the frames didn't bother me in the slightest.

A northeast breeze sent my reefer smoke down the beach. I could see Lobster Bob's umbrella crew working their way north. I hoped he caught a whiff. Busting pot smokers probably ranked higher on his list of life's joys than intercourse. Just a hint of marijuana wafting past sent him into RoboCop mode. I had to laugh picturing Bob busting ass up the beach following his nose.

I put the bone out against the bench's side and tucked it into my pocket to leave myself a little something for later. Behind me in the Lake Pavilion, Kim's Ice Cream Parlor opened. Just in time for a drink, I thought. During the day, Kim's does a nice business. With the public restrooms next door, it's like having a gas station just off the interstate. At night, though, a lot of little packets of white nose powder get bought and sold. That shit steals your humanity.

I got a large ice coffee to go. I sat on a bench facing Ocean Ave to people watch. Cars went by driven by guys wearing ties. How could somebody put on long pants, socks, stiff shoes, and a tie, then top off the torture with a ride along the beach before sitting in an indoor cubicle for eight hours?

"Fifty grand a year." The hell with later. "This one's for you," I took the bone out of my pocket and lit it as another dapper commuter drove by. I held it like a cigarette. No big deal. I washed down the roach with my coffee.

Looking up and down Ocean Ave, I tried to picture it thirty years ago. To the south, we had a movie theater—the Rialto. There was mini golf, a Stewart's Root Beer place, and an arcade with so many pinball machines their lights blinded you when you walked in from the dark. All kinds of places a teen could go. The roughest place turned out to be the arcade. If two kids wanted to fight, they'd meet there because they wanted an audience. There were always cops nearby. They would break it up in no time.

Bathhouses were big. One sat right next to J's corner, the Lipp's place. People drove down from the city in street clothes and needed a place to change and shower. Unlike Loch Arbour Beach, public beaches had no lockers. The bathhouse owners had pull with the borough council, and the town put up signs in the public restrooms that warned "No Disrobing" or "No Changing." The town would need twenty more cops to enforce that brilliant law. Instead, they counted on people's modesty and installed pay toilets.

I jerked around when a thumb poked my ear.

Vinny's high-pitched laugh drowned out the traffic. "See the mutha fucka jump?" he managed between hysterics.

Ronny's tanned face smiled down at me. "Couldn't resist. I saw Robin last night. She wants to see you, talk to you about your clinic or doctor visit."

"Doctor. Okay." I'd thought of it. Robin made the appointment. She knew the office personnel. If she could get an appointment that soon, could she see the scan results?

"How'd you make out? Going to be around a while?"

"Absolutely. Got work today." I reached into my backpack, pulled out those sunglasses, and put them on. "What do you think?" I held out a hand. "Foster Grant, baby."

"Very nice," he chuckled. "Glad you're okay." He steered his bike toward the boardwalk ramp. "Hey," he turned back, "guard party tonight on Chester. You remember? Same place as on the Fourth."

I lifted my hand. "I remember."

"Don't bring a date," Vinny said. He waited for Ronny to ride down the ramp, and together they pedaled north, Ronny sitting back, hands dangling at his sides, his shoulders squared as if an invisible brace framed them wide and straight.

That morning the clouds stayed inland in a long, flat ridge—mountain peaks in the distance. I noticed Mr. Kelly's dance bar parking lot filling up. Must be some kind of big luncheon, I figured. Kids in dark shorts and white golf shirts set up yellow wooden traffic fences to block off the lot. Soon the cars waiting to enter idled in a line. The people getting out of the cars looked old. Men in white shoes and paisley slacks hitched up over pot bellies, women taking small quick steps in their heels across the macadam.

At Mercer gate across from home, I didn't see my upstairs neighbor on his balcony. I thought I saw his walker through the railing, but a haze clung to my sunglasses. By that time, lunch hour had come and gone along with my bone and Kahlua buzz. The afternoon brought voice-whisking gusts—I put away my EL. The clouds that huddled inland all morning decided to make a trip east, and the afternoon turned to autumn as if August left early.

My last stop was Inlet. The way Annie sets up her gate, you can't see her coming from the south. She fastens a tarp across that side of her space to help block the wind. Today the tarp clung tight to the storm fence—all the air blew from the northeast.

Just as I got close enough to see she wasn't there, my heart did a double gainer when Highspire banged shut the lid of the storage bin.

"Jimmy!" He gave me the stink eye. "I got a problem with you." Strolling from the sand, he stopped at the shower's concrete base to rinse his feet, and then paraded up the ramp to Annie's gate.

"Where's Annie?" I mouthed.

"At the rest room. I'm checking badges. Know what else I'm checking?"

"Is this a riddle?"

Both hands on his hips, he leaned toward me. "Did you open that bin this morning?"

"To set up Annie's spot."

"That's what I thought. You left it open, padlock dangling. It didn't even look locked."

A family with small kids came walking toward the gate. I waved hello and took out a handful of Blow Pops from my backpack.

After they passed, Highspire snapped, "We're missing sweats, at least one torp, and all our extra lines."

"Leave me alone." It takes a lot of air to speak without my EL. I felt like a balloon flying around a room. I stopped for a breath. Highspire looked south, muttered something, and jogged toward the stand.

A few minutes later, Annie sang, "Hello, Jimmy." She wore her yellow sundress and a white cardigan she held with two hands at her throat. "Oh, this wind. I just need my house keys and for my ride to come."

I stood up and gave what there is of her a hug with my wrists. I had my voice in one hand and Blow Pops in the other. "Highspire's on my case."

"About the bin? I told him to forget about it. They were old sweatshirts, and no one's going to miss that buoy thing. They have extras down in the first aid warehouse." A white car pulled up to the boardwalk street ramp. "There's my ride, my nephew. See you in an hour, Jimmy," Annie waved. She stepped down the ramp, climbed in, waved once more, and smiled. She hadn't noticed my sunglasses.

The nephew put it in reverse and damn near clipped a car heading north. That car blew its horn along with the next two or three that passed. Between honks I heard her before I saw her, yapping away to her friends, her voice riding on a fresh gust.

"We been following you," Linda sang. She wore my Belmar Subs sweatshirt.

Ashley and Jill tagged a half-step behind. Towels around their shoulders, they walked their bikes to the storm fence, leaned them up against it, and took bike locks from their backpacks.

"You girls don't need to do that," I shook my hand. "Nobody's going to touch your bikes."

"Is Billy down there?" Linda lifted a pointer. "Holy moly. What's with those shades, mister?"

"Like them? They're my celebration glasses."

"I don't know about you, Jimmy. What are you celebrating?"

"Yesterday. I had my doctor visit."

"Oh, yeah! I knew it."

"So is Billy down there?" Jill piped up. She wore a two-piece. Ashley wore shorts and a long T-shirt. Jill carried her towel. Ashley had hers folded under crossed arms.

"He's down there. Are you cold?" I pointed at Ashley.

Jill smiled, "Ashley's always cold."

"Bullshit!" Ashley said. She looked at Linda when she spoke.

"Come on," Linda pulled Jill's bare arm.

They skipped down the ramp. Clouds passed overhead throwing shadows across the sand as they headed down the beach. Along the horizon, blue sky pinched between stretched, white-gray clouds as distant white caps surrounded the broad backs of Cooper and Harris up on the stand.

The girls walked to Billy's side of the stand. Linda went around the front and smacked Billy's foot. She spoke to him, looking up, then stepped aside and stood behind Jill and Ashley. A minute later, Ashley stepped aside.

Highspire's head and then his shoulders came up the tide rise from the water. Billy made a few gestures, and before I could give out Blow Pops to three kids, he traded places with Highspire and stood on the sand talking—arms folded in the casual lifeguard pose—to Jill.

Linda and Ashley peeled away, and Billy and Jill walked together down the tide rise until I could just spot the top of Billy's head. I pictured them talking away, the waves washing up the beach before retreating, the sand's wet shine drying before the next rush of foam.

The two collaborators skipped their way back to my gate. Up the ramp they came, arm in arm. "Oh, Jimmy," Linda laughed, "You missed it."

"Aaa, where do you go to school? What's your favorite subject?" mocked Ashley in a deep voice. "What a fuckin' scream! The boy is brainless!"

"Seventeen and eighteen. That okay for an age difference, Jimmy?"

I shrugged and smiled.

Linda had her hair gathered on one side in a ponytail. The wind whipped it back and forth. "No time for summer heartbreak so close to summer's end." She and Ashley picked up their bikes, turned south, and headed for the boardwalk ramp. Linda called back, "Watch out for her. I mean Jill."

By the time Annie's nephew dropped her off, I was done for the day. Already packed, I felt so free I could have cried. Watching Annie climb out of the car and walk up the boardwalk steps, Fridays from decades ago swept across my memory. A thousand weekends, a thousand Fridays looking forward to something big. So what if nine times out of ten the something big fell flat on its ass? Even when I worked for the DPW, knowing I'd be back at work Saturday morning didn't put a damper on Friday night.

I knew my plans for this Friday before I reached my apartment. It was as if Ronny had thrown a gauntlet at my feet. I saw myself in some over-budgeted, sword-clanging movie with damsels, knights, and wizards. First, a phone call to the princess.

"Hello, Robin."

"Jimmy! What a nice surprise. How did your doctor's visit go? Are you calling with good news?"

"Only doctors call with bad news."

"Oh, Jimmy. So what's the scoop? Did you see Dr. Edwards?"

"Yup. I saw everybody, and they saw me."

"Okay. And?"

I threw out names and repeated recommendations—those don't change whether you're fit or fodder. I bet I yakked for five minutes. "That's about it," I finished.

"Well, that's great. Super."

"I'd like us to celebrate. I'd like to take you out for a bite. On me. To show my appreciation." I hoped she didn't say super again.

"You don't need to do—"

"I know you're free. I still hear about guard parties."

"You are something."

"Around eight?"

"Eight it is."

I hung up. My hands shook when I held them out straight. I fixed myself a nice screwdriver in my Burger King Yankee cup and went into the bathroom to clean up. For a few seconds, summer smiled at me in the mirror, and I smiled right back. I had me a summer plan.

As I mentioned, in my trip to see Mrs. Toner at Belmar Public library, I learned about something wonderful in Ireland—the Burren.

The Burren lies in the northwest part of County Clare. It's a mass of rocky limestone that rises to heights and continues for miles. There is little else—no regular land or bodies of water. In 1649, Cromwell invaded Ireland. Trying to kill Catholics in God's name, Cromwell remarked that the Burren did not have water enough to drown a man, wood enough to hang one, or earth enough to bury him.

Yet as barren a place as it may look in winter, in the spring the Burren flora jumps to life. Unique and various ecological species grow side by side—plants from sea level grow alongside arctic-alpine specimens. Theories exist to explain this. Light density, the warm currents of the Gulf Stream carrying seeds from distant lands, the heat of the limestone.

Whatever the explanation, mysticism dwells about the place as if at any moment, a revelation will lend itself to anyone patient enough to wait and observe with a clear, objective eye. Nature is remarkable in her efforts to find new ways to create and sustain life. Men often take a different path.

12

TWO THINGS STUCK out in my thoughts like a Speedo on a fat man: don't bring up doctors; don't forget your summer plan.

For a location, I had making magic at Mebbe's in mind. Robin liked seafood. What could go wrong?

I pulled up outside her cottage. Lisa gave me a wave from the porch. She sure loved it out there. Maybe she spent time carving her initials on her gymnast railing. In high school, I carved sister sucks on a chair seat in Sister Mary Catherine's study hall—there wasn't enough chair top between my legs to carve sister Mary Agnes sucks. If Sister Mary Catherine thought someone meant her, oh well.

Some people may say only kids do that sort of thing. I disagree. As human beings, we carve our initials along the paths of our lives. We give rings to mark emotional commitment, stake out property on which to build or plant, start businesses to secure and increase our finances. We become bosses, Congressmen, priests, or lawyers and get more initials from churches, clubs, and political parties. Bullshit can and will pile up.

That was my summer plan. I wanted to carve some initials, and I wanted Robin to help. I gave her the layout—one location in two shifts—one full day's work.

"Let me get all that straight. You want me to what?" she laughed in the Caddy.

"Next Tuesday. Give me a morning or afternoon. I'll get Linda for whichever you don't want, and we'll do some planting."

"Flowers."

"Perennials. There's a difference. Along with some shrubs."

"At your daughter's house."

"Yup."

We drove past Silver Lake where Robin and Ronny fed the ducks back in June. "Where exactly did you and Ronny feed the ducks that night before you danced at the Lake Pavilion?"

She craned her head up and looked at the lake as we drove.

"There, I think," she pointed. "I remember the bench was behind us to our left."

"That's where Ronny stood when he tossed you his room key."

She looked at me. Her mouth turned down at one corner, eyes narrowed. "You are spooky sometimes."

"He told me all about tossing it to you, not the exact spot," I laughed. Damn phlegm. I had to pull over and stop.

"What did Edwards say about all that congestion?"

Shit. "I only cough when I laugh. I didn't laugh in his office." I lost my cool. After I finished clearing things, I threw the tissue in the street and slipped the Caddy into drive.

"Jimmy—"

I hit the brake, rifled the gearshift back to park, opened my door and picked up the damn tissue. "There," I tucked it next to my power seat switch and pulling out. "All fixed."

I loved watching Robin's eyes when we walked in Mebbe's. She looked around at the signs the way a kid looks at the bulletin boards first day at Kindergarten.

"Same items on each wall. Everything's fried except for the tarter and cocktail sauce."

Robin read, "Baked Alaskan king crab salad on toasted bun. Sandwich, platter.

"Forgot about that one."

"What's the platter?"

I pointed, "Fries and slaw. Lots and lots of fries."

"What about burgers and dogs? Are they fried?"

"Burgers no. Dogs sure. Cook that skin to a nice, crisp bite. They get finished on the grill."

Mrs. Mebbe and her upper-arm shimmy jiggled from fryer to counter to register. All five feet of her hustled. I caught Robin looking her over. A ripped seam ran from her moo-moo's armpit to the mid-ribs. Old, map-shaped grease stains blended into its faded floral print, and her white apron wore two soiled trails from thigh to knee where she constantly wiped her hands.

We decided to split a bucket of steamers. Murray served it up in his spotless white T-shirt and apron.

We were not the only people in Mebbe's. Two guys whose hands looked as if they had spent the day changing oil filters and sparkplugs sat at the picnic table next to us. They wolfed down dogs, fries, and burgers. Three teen boys sat down from us munching fries, and an elderly couple sat down to plan their attack on a bucket of steamers. With slow sober movements napkins, paper plates, broth, and butter were placed just so.

I nodded in the couple's direction and mouthed, "Watch them."

Robin glanced over as the lady selected her first clam. The shell dropped onto the paper plate. She peeled back the foot's skin. It joined the shell. Her thumb and forefinger held the morsel, swirled it in the broth, and dipped it in the butter. She made a big deal of it, holding it up for her hubby to see before dropping it in her mouth and smiling.

I didn't give Robin the how-to lesson I gave Linda—Ronny had taken care of that. She ate maybe five steamers. She let each one swim in the broth long enough for her fingers to prune. I stopped watching her after a time and got down to some serious eating. I like peeling three, pinching them all together and going right for the butter. I don't touch steamer to broth. That I drink down at the end.

I crumpled up my last napkin. "All set?"

"Don't they give you those little wipe things in the packet?"

I smiled, got up, and brought more napkins. I think the combination of the mechanic's hands and Mrs. M's splotched moo-moo did Robin in.

"Would you like to go somewhere for something else? Are you still hungry?" We were in the Caddy.

"I'm fine, Jimmy." She looked across the street.

I pulled into F Street traffic heading south. "I know where we can get barbeque chicken and have a cold beer."

"Where? Look at the people waiting outside Evelyn's."

I waited for her to figure it out. It only took a block.

"Not the guard party, Jimmy."

"We can just drop by."

"You're pushing the envelope."

"There's a good chance I'll get my ass kicked if I show up alone," I kidded.

Robin didn't see it that way. "You want me for insurance."

I hate driving and talking at the same time. F Street lights, crosswalks, bike riders—too much to look out for. That evening, I gave Robin a commencement speech.

We stopped for a red light. I began to tell Robin about Sophie and me, how and why we split. I told her about my night at Ed's with the seventh-grade girls. I told her about Denny and me. I left out names. I labeled—this guy, my friend, my wife. I told her I knew I'd loved the people I'd loved. I told her I loved her.

I drove to the end of Belmar and kept driving into Spring Lake. I drove through Sea Girt, past Alice's house. I saw the girls playing in the backyard on their new playhouse-slide thing. I turned around and drove back to Belmar, this time along Ocean Ave.

Along the way, Robin looked straight ahead. Only she knows if she listened.

I had my hopes for Tuesday clenched tight when I pulled up outside Robin's place. I kept the Caddy in the middle of the street. I didn't want awkwardness, her waiting for me to come around and open a door, me walking her up to the porch steps.

"We still on for Tuesday?"

"Sure, Jimmy. Don't go to that party," she touched my voice arm.

"I'll call you Monday to see which shift you want, a.m. or p.m."

The sunset reached pink across the rooftops as I watched her walk up the stairs, open the screen door, and go inside. Fucking insurance! It was a tad late for insurance. At least I got everything off my chest. She'd acted the perfect nurse.

Listening is a gift.

13

THE PARTY: A yard packed with red shorts and sweats, story-telling heads jerking and turning as if ducking from a hundred left jabs, raised voices sounding a single, off-key clamor, chicken-skin smoke riding a good northeast breeze down Chester all the way to Peggy's house one block down where I found a parking spot.

This time two guys sat on either side of a card table with a big metal cash box. They wore bright yellow T-shirts. So did two guys standing on either side of the seated pair—all middle age, heavy set, balding men except for one who looked even older.

"Twenty dollars, please," one of the seated guys said to me. He made me feel petite. His yellow belly bulged over the card table. "This is a benefit. Gail Cooper, a guard's little girl, needs to make a trip to Cleveland Clinic."

I gave the guy two twenties. "One for Gail."

"Thank you. Her daddy and grandpa appreciate it."

"I'm the grandpa," the older gentleman said. "Thanks very much."

I got my hand stamped—a red silhouette of a reclining, large-breasted woman. I've seen the same silhouette in chrome on an eighteen wheeler's mud flaps. I walked down the driveway toward the kegs thinking I should have worn my old wedding ring. Too bad. After Sophie and I split, I hocked it.

I spotted faces. Highspire, Harris, even the girl guard from Mercer. Casivette manned the chow. He paraded back and forth along both sides of three half oil drums flipping chicken quarters. He held a long pair of tongs and waved away smoke with his pith helmet. A gust swirled and he disappeared.

The spread looked impressive—nothing like the last party. Two long cafeteria tables end to end held big bowls of side dishes. Different kinds of potato salad, fruit salad, sliced cheeses, and meats. Big baskets of hard rolls, jars of pickles, olives, and artichoke hearts—everything wrapped tight in clear plastic wrap.

I drew a beer and found a corner of the yard without a cluster of guards standing together bullshitting. I counted three females without partners. Two other girls stood together trying to climb into each other's skin. Their heads swiveled around as if they were Christians in the Roman Coliseum.

As for his highness and faithful stooge, I didn't see either. Their orange gear would be hard to miss. I took my flask out from my pocket. It's a beautiful flask— polished pewter with an attached swivel cap. It had Powers Irish whiskey in it that night—the old man's brand. Drink a little courage, I think the saying goes.

Another beer, another sip. I kept moving. The more I watched, the more invisible I felt. The chicken looked damn good. Guards stood around the oil drums. One showed up with a paper plate. He may as well have banged the hell out of a dinner triangle.

Casivette smiled at the crowd, shook his head, moved on to turn another thigh and drumstick and repeated, "Not yet, goddamn it, not yet." After he turned his back, the chastised gathered at the abandoned end of the oil drums. Pilfering commenced.

Casivette turned, saw it, and called for reinforcements. "Jerry! Mr. Cooper!"

The grandpa in the yellow shirt came quick gimping along with the fat guy who took my money.

"Hey now! We'll let you know when, fellas," grandpa said. "Put 'em back, now," he motioned at two guards holding chicken. They looked fifteen. What faces. As if their sisters caught them jerking off.

Brother guards saw and chanted, "Douche-bags, douche-bags."

"Mind you—keep your eye on the one you picked," Jerry, the younger guy, cautioned. "That one's yours," he pointed. "Your fingers bought it."

After the crowd cleared, I wandered over.

"What's your problem?" Casivette grumbled.

"Got an extra set of tongs?"

He looked from me to a piece of chicken and back again.

"Do I know you?"

"I'm a gate guard here in Belmar."

He looked around. "Check over there on that table," he pointed his pith helmet before bringing it back in front of his face and waving himself.

I found a pair. They were flimsy and shorter than Casivette's, but what the hell. I started turning chicken.

"Just follow me." Casivette looked at my tongs. "I'll get the ones in the middle. You cover the edges." A born direction-giver.

A gave him a tong salute and flipped away. I never thought about what would happen when I got to the drums' west side. All that smoke—I doubled over and stumbled out of it. For a minute, it felt like I'd coughed up something permanent. Casivette had his back turned and didn't notice. I met him on the other side. He looked at me as if I'd disobeyed a direct order.

"What?"

"I can't get over there," I motioned across the drums and pointed to my stoma.

"Okay. Hey, aren't you Hopkins' friend? You were with him in White's that day. After he hurt his foot."

I gave him the okay and nodded.

Casivette turned a quarter and shook his head. "Hopkins doesn't think much of you, does he? It's none of my business, and frankly I don't care either way."

I got right next to him. "I remember when you worked on Waterfront. I used to come to your beach. I bet you weighed one-thirty soaking wet."

"One-fifty. I carried my weight in my ass. How old are you?"

"Forty-seven."

"I got five on you. I was on Waterfront five, six years."

"It was my father's beach. I went there until he died. It didn't feel the same after."

He looked me up and down. "Yeah, well. Back to the chicken."

We made it around one time. We stepped back away from the coals— they cranked out the heat—and took big swigs of our beers. Grandpa Jerry brought us two fresh ones.

I stuck the tongs under my arm. "Thank you. You're Mr. Cooper?"

"Yes."

"I know a Sam Cooper from Inlet Ave."

"My son. His little girl, three years old, Gail. She's the star today. She needs a heart valve repair," he touched his chest. "Cleveland Clinic is very good. Highly recommended. And you are?"

"Jimmy Hanlon." I couldn't shake. I was out of hands. Mr. Cooper saw my problem. He gripped my wrist and squeezed it.

"Thanks again, Jimmy. How long, John?"

"Ten, fifteen minutes," Casivette puffed. Sweat ran down his cheeks.

After Mr. Cooper left, I said to Casivette, "Did you know Ireland gets about an inch further away from Jersey every year? They were part of the Old Red Sandstone Continent about two million years ago."

He looked at me and circled his tongs in the air. "Twice more around the barbeque continent, Jimmy. That's all we got left."

I wondered if Cooper's drunk and the problems with Denise back in June had anything to do with little Gail's troubles. Summer dust under someone else's rug. I didn't look at it that way. Instead, I saw another example of my ignorance. Summer does that, too. You can walk the sand in another's footprints and never realize it.

I welcomed contradiction that day. I saw my summer as one long journey of exploration instead of some doctor-declared absolute. Ronny supplied gas, Robin a destination, Peggy a lot of detours, Antony and Linda roadmaps. All I had left was the finish—Alice. First, though, I had to get through the party in one piece.

I passed Casivette in sweat production. When he declared the chicken was done, I gave up my tongs and worked myself through the crowd to the enclosed outside shower on the side of the house halfway down the driveway. I put my voice on the highest shelf, turned on the cold water, and cupping my hand over my stoma, stuck my head under the stream. Man, that felt good. I didn't see a towel, so I stuck my ass out to keep my pockets dry for my voice.

A long line of red welcomed me from the shower—first and only time I ever saw lifeguards stand in single file. Cooper saw me. He stood in line along with everybody else. He held out a hand.

"My father told me about your extra donation. Thanks a lot, Jimmy." Each word his arm-piston pumped me hard enough to knock me back. Good thing he didn't let go of my hand.

I waved thanks and moved on to the keg—no sense not taking advantage of the food line. I settled down under the only tree in the yard—a big swamp maple with two thick distinct trucks. Since there weren't chairs or tables, the guards stood and devoured chicken before grabbing a plate and moving on to the side dishes.

Somebody called out, "Did the track team pay up?" I scanned the line and caught Highspire dropping his hands from his mouth. Four abreast they came down the driveway, a line of orange rowing shorts and white and orange tank tops—Ronny, Vinny, Paulie, and Ted. Heads in the chicken line turned as they passed.

"They paid," Casivette called from the end of the driveway. He sat next to Cooper's dad. They both had plates in their laps.

It got spooky quiet. I heard the radio up in the second-floor window for the first time. Conversation in the line hushed as The Four Horsemen cut through on their way to the kegs. Ronny looked down at me and smiled as he passed.

"The benefit brought you, huh?"

"Jim-my," Paulie smiled.

Ted waved without looking at me.

Vinny snickered all the way to the keg.

After the chicken line shortened, I stood up and walked to the end. Highspire stood about four or five guards from the chicken.

"The Loch Arbour mascot," he pointed at me.

I had my beer in one hand, my voice in the other.

"You mean me, Highspire? I'm a mascot?"

"None other. Did you bring your checkbook to pay for those missing items?" His grin stretched wide.

"Fuck you."

My turn for the chicken—I found my old friendly tongs and reached for one of the last dozen or so pieces left on the wire grill. Most looked a little black. I spooned some potato salad alongside my chicken, picked a few cherry tomatoes from the tossed salad, and completed that side of my plate with a big ladle of baked beans—I love that sweet, bacon fat sauce on anything.

I settled in against the white fence between the party yard and the house to its east. I dug into the beans and potato salad first. I didn't want chicken fingers until all I had left was the chicken. A trash can sat up against the fence maybe ten feet down from me.

I had my legs folded under me, my plate in my lap. I picked up my chicken just as Highspire and two sidekicks came close with empty plates, I figured headed for the trash can. Highspire took a slight detour.

He walked past me, moved his hand up from his hip, and slapped away my chicken as I held it up to bite. It helicoptered down the driveway and skidded to a stop against some guard's flip-flop.

He didn't look down at me, didn't laugh.

"Faggot," he snickered.

He walked over to my chicken and picked it up. He inspected it as if it might come alive. Then he walked to a trash can and, holding the chicken at eye level, dropped it. He wiped his hands together, laughed, and walked away.

I waited a few minutes, sitting there. After everybody's eyes left me, I stood up and wandered. Everybody had finished eating. Smoke from the coals drifted up in little wisps each time the wind puffed hard. I kept track of Highspire. Ronny and his crew hadn't left the kegs. They weren't eating—just trying to drink twenty dollars' worth. I watched them drink a round.

I watched all four of them pull new beer into their cups. Then I walked to the trash can, picked out my dirt-covered chicken, snuck up to Highspire, and shoved that quarter piece right in his face just as hard as I could.

At contact, he yelled and twisted away. I'd surprised him and backed him up a step. He looked at me, a war paint-line of grease and dirt across his cheek and forehead. His eyes opened wide at me, but all I could see was that black mushed chicken skin trail on his face, and I cracked up. I pointed at him and laughed my ass off.

Other guards started to point and laugh. The black smeared line started next to his nose, dropped a little, and then swooshed up to his temple and across his forehead. The sight of it tickled me more than anything else that summer.

The next thing I knew, Ronny stood between me and Highspire. With all the hooting and yelling, I didn't hear what he said. For every step Ronny took forward, Highspire took one back. Then Casivette, Mr. Cooper and son, and every yellow shirt came between the two of them. A second later, somebody yelled, and a path opened in the crowd to where more yellow shirts ran to a Belmar guard on the ground. Hands on his belly, his knees gently swaying side to side, they pulled him onto his feet. Somebody had snuck in a quickie.

A minute after that, with a yellow shirt on each shoulder, Ronny walked down the driveway. The other orange boys followed, and I took advantage of the confusion and hustled out of there.

Forty dollars for two beers, a half-hour of standing over a hot grill, some baked beans, and payback. Without a doubt the best forty bucks I ever spent.

I wanted to know just what the hell had gone on between Ronny and Highspire. I followed the orange boys on foot. With Estel's only a block down, I figured they had it in mind, and I guessed right.

For a Friday night, there wasn't much of a line out in front—probably because all the guards were at the benefit. I saw Ronny and the others in line. I crossed Ocean Ave to wait on a bench so it wouldn't look like I'd followed them.

Behind me, the sun dipped below the rooflines. The horizon looked ready for bed. It came together with the ocean in a tired, deep blue line. A few kids walked along the tide rise. One out in front of the others turned, backed up, then gestured and waved his arms as if introducing his followers to an undiscovered wonder. I tried to remember where my day would start tomorrow. I kept my schedule on the fridge, but I couldn't picture it. I couldn't picture anything except what stretched in front of me.

A car horn shook me. I got up, deserted my flip-flops, and headed down the Essex Ave ramp onto the sand. It felt cool on my feet. I walked past the tipped guard stand and boat all the way to the tide rise. There wasn't a dip on Essex like on Inlet—the wash inched up the sloped sand then paused before sliding back to the next wave.

I sat down crossed-legged, got my flask out, and drained it. I lit up a nice cigar, puffed it bright, and watched the smoke twist off its glow. Before me danced gentle green—no cloud shadows cast the surface bright or dark. The sea in evening attire—top hat and cane optional.

Streetlights along the boards had flicked on by the time I stood up and brushed the sand off my ass. A few party boats lit the water, dark now and only showing itself in broken swishes of white foam on shore. The breeze had turned damp. My hair felt stiff from the salt air.

Up over the boards I could see Estel's marquee, a big blob of white light sticking up over the traffic along Ocean Ave, "Scarlett Begonias Tonight" spelled in big red letters. Halfway to the boards, I could make out heads and then shoulders of people standing on the porch in line waiting to get in. Friday night still—anything goes.

I found my flip-flops, brushed off one more time, made sure I had voice, flask, wallet, and keys in the right pockets, and crossed Ocean Ave. I even tested the crosswalk—walked right out in front of a pair of headlights. I felt good enough to smack a hood.

In line I could hear the Begonias. I knew their sets. I caught myself lifting up on my toes to "Sugar Magnolia." "Mr. Charley" escorted me to the porch steps. I finished a cigar—halfway, at any rate—by the time I got on the porch.

Estel's was stuffed full. The Doorman had his counter clicking fast as a track coach's stopwatch during tryouts.

"Four out, four in. Go. One out—one in." A leg-thick arm stuck out straight, "One, not three!"

"But we're all together," one of the female threesome begged.

"One or none."

A quick conference. "We'll wait."

Hand up, big smile on my face, I pushed through to the front.

"I'm one," I held up a finger. Tony Stallion's giant paw pushed my scapula inside. I paid my cover—three bucks with a marquee band—and stepped into the rat race.

With the Begonias on break, Estel's bar had become a shrine with a horde of pilgrims trying to worship. Off in Estel's northwest corner stood the boys in fugitive-orange rowing shorts. Some guy rolled quarters into the jukebox. Before it came to life, I got the come-on wave from Ronny. He held out his beer for me to sip. I walked over and took it.

"Not afraid of catching something?"

They were the first and last words I spoke the entire time in Estel's to Ronny. The jukebox roared.

"I'm not worried," Ronny bent into my ear. He straightened and smiled. He held out a palm. I tucked away my voice and shook hands.

Vinny tilted back his head, lifted his beer bottle mic, and sang along with the bar, "I'm ya penis, I'm ya fire, at ya duh-zi-a!"

Paulie tapped my shoulder, pulled me in close. "You see me drop Donaldson?"

I shook my head no.

"A short left," he demonstrated. "I felt it go all the way to his kidneys." He leaned back and shrugged, smoothed his tsunami hair with a hand and smiled.

Vinny held up his beer to the crowd and moved it like a baton; Paulie pumped elbow to ribs; Ronny smiled his smile as his eyes flashed approval from one disciple to the next. When he looked back at me, he shook his head and leaned down again.

"I heard enough takes-one-to-know-one-shit the last few weeks. Maybe I found out a little about you."

I looked at him for a second before I handed back his beer.

"It took balls to show at the party."

I turned to the bar. A spot had opened. I took a step toward open space. I couldn't look him in the eye. I could have cried. I hustled into the fray, weaved my magic through and around, and leaned home against the bar, safe.

"Two Buds" I mouthed and held up my fingers.

Bodies filled in behind. I twisted this way and that and held tight with one hand on the rail edge while I drank with the other.

My night, boy. Four or five kids tilted back their beers, finished them off, set the bottles down on the window's counter, and headed for the exit. I sailed right up to the window with room on both sides to stretch my arms if I wanted.

In the window's reflection, I saw Ronny and the rest still standing in the corner. Out on the porch, the line moved up as the door gulped in that group of three girls who'd waited to get in. One looked around and shrieked as if she'd won the lottery.

As I said, my night. Shit aligned in the sky that Carl Sagan wouldn't comprehend. There she stood on the top step, just off the porch, bundled up in a red cardigan—Lisa. And behind her Robin, talking to two other girls. I recognized one—the robe and doggie-faced slippers girl who surprised Billy Harris and his pick-up date fornicating the night Ronny air-mailed Lisa over the porch railing. I had a front row seat to summer at its best.

A summer bar is one hell of a place for memories and plans to collide, and sometimes truth makes a lousy bumper. I didn't want Robin mentioning anything to Ronny about my doctor's visit. I figured the scarcer I made myself, the better the chances it wouldn't happen.

I gave up my share of the glass and ducked behind some tall bastard when he and his friends sidled up next to me. I didn't want Robin spotting me through the window. I knew how to stay hidden in a crowded bar.

By the time the four girls made it in, I'd managed to grab a barstool, an actual piece of furniture on which to sit. People stood on the small dance floor watching the Begonias get their act together for another set. Like most cover bands the Begonias had themselves a following—long hair on the guys and long dresses that swayed every which-way on the girls.

They started out slow. "Uncle John's Band" and "Fire on the Mountain." So did the collision. The two foursomes spotted each other across the bar. Ronny's stone face stuck above most of the bobbing deadheads. Robin smiled and pointed. Lisa's feet were stuck in glue. The other girls may as well have been standing in the check-out at Shop-Rite. Their eyes followed Robin as she crossed the bar, stood in the dance floor's middle, hands on hips, and tilted her head back in laughter.

Ronny grinned, took steps toward her, and gathered her up in his arms. Feet together, he turned her smile in a circle, the two of them a centerpiece of the big music box that was Estel's dance floor.

The L.A. boys scattered. Vinny headed for the bar. Before Ronny put Robin down, Paulie stood in front of Lisa. He held an arm out for her to follow him to a window spot. He pulled a stool out for Lisa, and she sat down, her smile intact. She didn't see, but I smiled with her.

August. You never know, Lisa, I wanted to tell her. Two months after you entered your first summer bar scared to death, there's a chilly evening, so you pull a red cardigan from its hanger in your closet. The next thing you know, you're seated at a picture window overlooking the Atlantic Ocean with a guy who an hour ago dropped a lifeguard with a sneaky left to the mid-section.

The Begonias hit "China Cat Sunflower." I'd miss "I Know You Rider." September follows August. Estel's held sway over all of us, from Stallion with his patron-clicker to Lisa with the cold bottle of Bud I bought her on my way out.

"Jimmy, thanks! Where are you going? Did you see Robin?"

"Home," I mouthed, nodding yes.

14

SATURDAY AND SUNDAY, the last weekend before Labor Day, played like two different records. Saturday spun a soulful slow dance—Percy Sledge, "When a Man Loves a Woman." Sunday howled and strutted "(I Can't Get No) Satisfaction."

Saturday morning, I got up early. Taking a long way to my first gate, I noticed signs of things to come.

First, I got a coffee and bagel from the Lipp—he looked giddy, gazing up at the clear blue sky, almost as if he was about to turn an Irish jig. Then I cut down to A Street and walked up to Silver Lake on my way to Essex. I walked all the way around the lake, something I hadn't done in years. Oh, I'd walked parts, but not intentionally just to see the sights.

The morning air had a September chill. Every dozen steps I caught myself rubbing my bare arm, then switching my coffee to the other hand and warming the other. The lake had a thin haze just above the surface, so the glass-smooth water seemed to lift without moving in the early morning light. In every shrub I passed, a half dozen cupped spider webs shimmered, dew-covered and heavy with wet. Yellow willow leaves and an occasional early-turned red maple spotted the ground. I kicked at them to hear an autumn sound, but they weren't dry enough to rustle. The birds on Ronny's father's island sanctuary ruffled feathers, waddled to the water, and swam toward me for some breakfast. I broke off a piece of bagel without cream cheese, closed my eyes, and tossed it. Five or six green necks sprinted to the spot.

"Only enough for one."

The borough boys had the grass and flower beds looking sharp. Rounding the end at C Street I couldn't see any open parking spots. Lots of people take vacation days late in August, so that was no surprise.

I stood at the Essex Ave gate and checked my watch—7:26. What I would do to kill an hour and a half didn't concern me. I knew when I woke up. Tuesday's work needed a plan.

I opened the Essex storage locker, took out a chair, and headed for the shoreline. Once I got down by the water, I faced the chair north and sat down to read my paper. That got the gray cells working. I had the left side all set— or is it the right? Whichever side controls creativity, it felt ready to go.

I took out the yellow legal pad I'd folded into the sports section and my color markers. A rough rectangle served for Alice's house. I drew the porch and her front steps more to scale—the house's front needed the overhaul—and then I drew in my planned beds.

Bill had done all the prior landscaping. I told Alice, "Marines don't landscape like this."

Alice told me, "I get the porch, Bill's got the yard."

"Fire him," I suggested.

He's about as creative as a parking meter. First, he had the front beds parallel with the front of the house. Five feet of plant material with landscape ties on the bed's border. I hate landscape ties. Might as well fly a white flag and stick in daffodil bulbs along their inside edge.

The front view of the house presented itself like soldiers. Two rows of equidistant marigolds lined up for a charge. The east and west corners of the beds were ninety degrees. One shrub stood at each corner—old yews that received a yardstick-guided trim every spring and fall. They looked like sentries. Bill should have decorated them with helmets on top and rifles alongside. The strait-laced bastard had them trimmed so tight they could've passed for solid green phone booths.

Behind the pawn marigolds, he'd lined up—I'm not kidding—six dwarf Alberta spruce. One stood every three feet. The first was three feet away from the corner yew, the last three feet from the porch. I measured. Three on one side of the porch, three on the other. He must have found them at a discount nursery because they were maybe eighteen inches tall. I figured if they all lived and grew at the same rate, they'd make six feet by the time Suzanne and Jessica had grandchildren.

The east corner was a lost cause. Next to the attached garage, it needed a large-scale, snaking dig line from mid-driveway up to the front walk. Anything with curves. It would have taken too much of everything—time, effort, and money.

The west corner, though—that could be saved. First, the ties had to go. Then we'd start at the front walk, dig out a few feet, then gently curve back to the center—we'd just return to the existing border for a foot or so—and sweep out again to the corner. A simple half-circle would finish the digging. Not too bad. We'd turn the sod over, cover it with newspaper and match Bill's mulch. He used pine bark. Not my favorite, but easy to find.

I drew the new bed line on my legal pad. Now to fill in my space. The corner yew had to go along with the next spruce. At least that made five across. Something low with color to replace the spruce and start to fill the half circle…three blue star juniper. They'd guide the eye. Next some mixed color. Three of each: Gaillardia in the front for spring, planted off the junipers; then for summer a mix of purple coneflowers and Shasta daisies at the back. To hold everything together in the semi circle's center, a full, gold columnar. Chamaecyparis might work. I hoped my buddy Phil at Hallow Brothers Nursery had a nice selection.

When I finished making squiggle circles for the plants, I knew I had to do something about the marigolds. I decided to throw in a few lamb's ears to break it up for the present. Next spring Alice could decide what else she wanted to mix in—maybe some sage if she liked the blue-purple thing I'd started. Even if she repeated the marigold columns, at least the lamb's ears would break them up—they spread like crazy. For the east side I planned three rudbeckias. They and the coneflowers re-seed.

I totaled up a guestimate. It all came to close to two hundred bucks, depending if I went with #1's or #2's on the blue stars. For the columnar, I'd have to get at least #4. The perennials might be half price this time of year.

All day at my gates, I pulled out the pad and re-worked my drawing. I figured how many shovelfuls I had to dig. I used each line on the paper as one foot. Knowing my digging spade measured eight inches across, I came up with a rough total.

"You're turning into Bill," I laughed at myself.

What the hell. Robin or Linda would be there to talk to during the breaks, and I had all day. I was off. Alice, Bill, and the girls would be in Cape May from Monday until Thursday morning. I had plenty of time.

Who the hell lives two blocks from the beach and drives hours to celebrate his wife's birthday at the same ocean, different sand? Bill. Cape May's where his parents took him growing up, so that's where he takes Alice and the girls for three weekdays because the B&B rates climb up Thursday-Sunday. An authentic cheap bastard.

Saturday, I ended the day at Inlet. Annie skipped her break. We talked for her entire hour. She stayed in her chair and worked on a cross-stitch of a beach scene while I leaned in under her umbrella, nice and cozy.

"Have you seen Alice?"

"Talked to her last Sunday."

"How are the girls?"

I kept one eye on Highspire. Sitting on the stand, every minute or so he glanced over his shoulder. I didn't know why. I started to think he was waiting for Annie to leave.

"Full of salt and vinegar as usual."

"Isn't that pee and vinegar?" Annie smiled.

I smiled back. "I think so."

"That boy down there," Annie motioned at the guard stand. "He has some mouth on him. He doesn't much care for you."

"Which?" I knew she meant Highspire, and I could guess what he'd been saying.

"That one up top."

Highspire sat alone on the stand. I recognized Billy standing alongside. "Cooper's summer finished last week, right? How's his little girl?"

"They're hopeful she'll be okay, he told me." She never took her eyes off the cross-stitch. "Jimmy?"

She paused long enough for me to wonder if I'd hear the question. Is it true? That you're…that you prefer…

"Right here," I touched a finger to her cross-stitch near two flying seagulls.

"What?"

"More seagulls. You need another couple," I touched two spots back and forth. "Odd numbers always look better."

"Well, I was thinking couples. Oh, I wanted to ask if you'd visited your daughter. After your dinner, I got the feeling, just a feeling, that Alice wanted you to drop by. Not call ahead. Just drop by. Right after dinner's always a good time."

I had to chuckle inside. I'd shivered at the tone of my name being spoken, felt my chest tighten with indignation before the fact. I won't lie. The healing's ongoing. I didn't carry a support group poker chip in my pocket.

"How about coming with me?"

She kept up with her cross-stitch, then almost in a singsong, "I have a feeling your daughter just wants you to show up. I'd be a distraction."

"You're right, damnit. Darn it," I smiled.

She looked up at me over her glasses. "I think so. Tomorrow's Sunday. You phone her on Sundays. Am I right?"

Annie really got herself rolling. For a good five minutes, she reminded me of things Alice had said at our Lughnasa dinner. How Alice recalled me renting that shitty apartment so I could watch her walk to and from school. How she remembered the player's name on the bat she got when I took her to bat day.

"Tom Tresh. Alice called him Tommy. Maybe she had a crush on him. Who knows? But she still loves the man who took her to that game." She let her cross-stitch drop to the boardwalk. "Do you hear what I'm saying, Jimmy Hanlon?"

"Loud and clear."

"Here comes big britches. Don't engage him."

Always on camera, Highspire walked toward the gate, his steps as deliberate as a father of the bride. I handed Annie my voice.

Highspire stopped at the storage bin. He opened it, gazed in—I couldn't see him except for a hand on the lid's top—then after a few seconds, slammed it shut. A final parting stare at yours truly, and he retreated to his stronghold.

"Well," Annie huffed, "not a sound out of him. That is a first."

I motioned for my voice. Annie watched Highspire walk away. I had to tap her shoulder.

"Oh," she handed it to me. "I have a feeling somebody had words with him."

"Somebody I'd know?"

"Somebody who showed up this morning on his bicycle on his way north." Annie smiled a smile I'd never seen before—tight and toothless.

"You swallow a canary?"

"Oh, I didn't hear," she showed teeth. "The two of them were halfway to the water. But I saw that boy's face melt onto his chin. Wild gestures, pointing. All the other guards stood around the stand watching. I don't think they wanted to miss something."

I craned my head sideways like a dog hearing a fire siren. "How about you, Annie Thompson? I suppose you kept your head down and worked on your cross-stitch."

"Not on your life. I was hoping Ronny would deck him."

14

WORK ON SUNDAY lingered long and slow. As I walked home after my last gate stint, I spotted a nice surprise. It was Linda. I was going to call her later that evening. Now I wouldn't have to. On top of a beach towel, she sat on my little stoop. Legs crossed at the ankles, she leaned back on an elbow and lifted a cigarette to her lips. With her sunglasses, big hair, and one of those outfits with crazy day-glow colors and a tutu bottom, she looked like someone out of a music video. I don't watch MTV videos, but occasionally I catch one while I'm channel surfing.

"'Bout *time*," she complained.

I walked further so she'd hear me. "Some of us have jobs. Why a Saturday visit? Not that I'm complaining."

"News update."

She hopped up, shook the towel like a dusty throw rug, threw it over one shoulder, and came alongside me.

"What's the news?" I unlocked the door and opened it for her. "Be right up." I reached for my mailbox as she sped upstairs. A Shop-Rite flyer, my *Time* magazine, and one very bright white envelope from the oncology clinic. I opened it and read. The light was good—I didn't even have to stretch my arm out.

It was about my coming appointments. Date, time, and place. Treatments. Follow ups. A strict schedule of conventional nonsense. I'd put summer in charge of my itinerary. She'd never given me a printed list.

Halfway up the stairs I heard the opening of "Sugar Pie Honey Bunch." The kid had caught on.

I twisted a hand for her to turn it down.

"Thank you. Now, what's your news? You want a Pepsi?"

She left the turntable and stood right in front of me, hands behind, her eyes looking up and impish smile growing. "This might require a beer."

I shook my head. "I shouldn't have given you that last one." At the fridge I got myself a Pabst and popped her open a Pepsi. I sat on the sofa and patted the other side. "Come on," I held out her soda.

"Well," she flopped down, bouncing a leg under her. She unloaded gum from her mouth, stuck it on her knee, and took her Pepsi. "Here goes. It seems that Ronny bought Margaret a truck that—"

"I've seen it."

"Do you want to hear this or not?"

"Please continue."

"Ronny bought Margaret a truck. Except he didn't. Last night he returned it."

"He returned it?" I played along. Holy shit—he didn't even wait until Labor Day.

"All I know is that last night a man picked it up and took it. He had the keys, all the signed papers from Ronny. Mom flipped. She pulled soup cans and noodle boxes out from the cupboards. The floor still looks like an earthquake hit."

"Let's go out on the balcony."

I wanted to light a cigarette, open my beer, and pull the string on one of those pop-streamer things. I tried not to laugh, but as soon as I sat down outside, I exploded. I leaned forward. Bent at the waist, I sucked in air, laughed it out, and howled like a lunatic.

"What?" Linda chuckled.

Then she lost it. She had to hold on to the railing. People walking past on the sidewalk looked up at us and pointed. I had to put my arms up over my head to keep from choking. I laughed and coughed so hard I brought something up in my mouth and had to run inside to spit. Linda started to follow me, but I shook my head and held a hand back behind me.

I closed the bathroom door.

"Jimmy, are you okay?" she kept saying.

I took care of things, splashed water on my face. Those black dots spun around in front of my face in the mirror. My hands tight on each side of the sink, I waited for everything to calm down. Then I flushed the toilet, opened the door, and made straight for the vodka.

"You look white."

I held up my hand, smiled, and fingerspelled a-ok.

Back on the balcony with my drink and Linda, we sat down, took deeps breaths, and started up again.

"Ronny rented a truck, let Margaret drive it thinking it was hers, and then had it picked up out from under her." Linda pursed her lips and nodded, "It came as quite a shock to mother."

"Was Ronny there? Are you upset by the whole thing?

"Nope and nope."

Down below in the street two boys on bikes with stingray handlebars tried to out-wheelie each other.

"That is too bizarre for words."

"I know why he did it."

So did I. I also did not want to discuss it. Linda looked down at the boys. They were ten or eleven. Every time the one kid did a wheelie over the curb, he made engine-revving sounds.

"He got that car so Margaret wouldn't go after him. For me. For him and me."

"I've told you before. It wasn't your fault."

"It sure wasn't yours. Or theirs," she pointed down at the two boys. "Their bikes are bigger than mine."

Summer regrets near its end.

"You've done a lot of growing up."

She turned away and looked out at the dance bar parking lot. It was still full. Nobody in the Osprey wanted to call it a weekend.

"It'll be okay. You can't do anything about the two of them except not to let them get to you. You have school coming, all your friends."

"Some friends. Some turned into something else. Oh, shit. What about Antony's friends? They all hate me. They'll say that's my fault. Everything's my fault. Oh, shut up!" Linda called to the two boys on bikes.

They ignored her. They rode down Mercer, peddled like crazy, then turned and whooped as they hopped the parking lot curb and side-skidded to a stop just before smashing into the car at the end of a row.

"Antony wasn't your fault. I lost friends this summer too. We're leftovers, you and me," I pointed back and forth at us.

"Shit. It's all so boring," she sighed. My heart melted for her.

"Hey," I perked up, remembering the planting. "How about helping me plant some flowers Tuesday? I was going to call and ask you tonight."

"Plant flowers?"

"Tuesday's my day off. I'm working all day at Alice's house planting flowers as a surprise for her birthday. They're going to be away, so that's planting day. Robin's helping too. You can take the morning or afternoon shift. I'll pay you ten bucks an hour."

"Ten Bucks?"

"Cash."

She put her head down. A finger ran around the rim of her soda can. One of the boys down below lifted too hard on his handlebars, and over he went, right on his ass as the bike tipped back and smacked the blacktop beside him. He was right in the middle of an impressive string of obscenities directed at his companion when I looked down the street and saw they weren't the only two bikes on Mercer.

"Go inside," I told Linda. She saw the same thing I did. She didn't ask why.

The two rode up onto the front walk, straddled their bikes, smiled, and waved up.

"What's going on?" Ronny called.

"I have no idea."

"Throwing my line back at me." He looked around. The two boys were listening.

"Take off!" Vinny got off his bike and walked toward them waving his arms. They skedaddled.

"You have anything extra in your freezer, Jimmy?"

I leaned way over the balcony railing and waited for a car to pass to make sure he could hear me. "This isn't a hostel in Amsterdam."

He nodded and smiled. "How's Highspire been treating you lately?"

"Just fine."

"That's good to hear."

"You two had a talk. Annie told me."

"A couple."

"Why can't you be an anonymous good guy?"

"C'mon," Vinny said, back on his bike, "we're gonna be late."

"Twenty bucks for a couple of bones. C'mon, Jimmy."

"Tell them to wait down there," Linda hissed at me from inside.

I held up a finger to the borstal boys and went inside. "What?"

Linda held a hand over the phone. I came alongside her, and she took off her hand and whispered, "Right now! He's waiting for Jimmy to give him some smoke." She nodded her head and then hung up.

I looked at her after she let go of the receiver.

"Margaret's riding my bike over," she smiled. "You should have heard her. This is going to be way cool."

I had a hard time keeping a straight face. "I'm not tossing joints off my balcony."

"So invite them up. I'll stay in the spare room. Keep them in the living room."

She sounded like Barbara Stanwyck in the grocery store in *Double Indemnity*—matter of fact, colder than her already dead husband. I didn't know whether to scold or congratulate her.

Later, after all the nonsense and before I received a late-night caller, two things stuck in my mind. I remembered I hadn't called Alice to wish her happy birthday in advance before their mini vacation. I didn't blame myself, though. No wonder with all the shit that went on. The second thing sank its talons into my brain and wouldn't let go. It kept me lying awake in the dark gazing at my mural, listening to cars along Ocean Ave swoosh past in puddles. How had I missed that side of Linda? She had the same swagger as the rest of them. Fashionable chest-thumping that the 80's passed out as carelessly as 5 for $1 beers at Ray's—look good while getting even. What the hell—I let it happen.

Out on the balcony I gave the okay sign and waved up Vinny and Ronny. They bounded up the stairs. I turned on TV, got my freezer stash, and stood over the kitchen counter with my Zig Zags.

"Grab a beer," I tossed my head at the fridge.

They grabbed and sat as if they were two kids in the principal's office. Not a how are you or go to hell. Not a single remark. I went to work—double papers. Those babies looked like two perfect Pall Malls without ink on the paper when I finished.

They had TV tuned to some movie on channel eleven. The two of them sat on the couch, sipped their beers, and watched without speaking. I went around in front of them, exaggerated my posture as if Patton called me to attention, and holding a bone in each hand, crossed my arms at the wrists.

"Gentlemen, your weapons."

"Oh, shit," Vinny said.

"Thanks Jimmy."

"You're welcome. I shall be out on the veranda," I tried to sound like a butler. After all, I was serving them up.

I took my drink out and sat down. I left the slider open to share the cool, late August evening.

The occasion called for a cigar. I fired up one of my anisette-flavored stinkers. Inside the Freak Brothers toked up a fog bank. It wasn't my dope from June. This dope you didn't smoke before discussing current events. This dope kicked serious ass. About the only thing I could do on it was sit out on the balcony and watch the night sky for satellites.

I'd had one sip of screwdriver and two puffs on my cigar when I spotted the funnel cloud pedaling down Ocean Ave. Peggy stood a good head taller than Linda. She had longer legs, and those gams pointed out like chicken wings as that bike swiveled side to side. She turned down Mercer, and after she picked up momentum, lifted her feet off the pedals, stretched her legs out straight and coasted. As she jumped the curb and let the bike drop to the sidewalk, our eyes locked.

She smiled—a hellion at play. She put a finger to her lips. I lifted the hand holding my cigar and nodded. Her stare could have burned a hole in the building. It occurred to me to close the slider. For some reason, all the anticipation I'd felt for this collision evaporated. I left the slider open a crack.

My guests were still on the couch. I didn't see a bone going—just the two of them sitting.

Ronny lifted a beer to his lips just as the top door flew open. Peggy stood in the doorway, hands on hips—Wonder Woman confronting Nazis. Even the TV hushed. Vinny uncrossed his legs. Feet planted, hands on thighs, his ass grew off the couch.

"I gotta go," he announced.

"What? What for?" Ronny deadpanned.

"I just remembered."

"Remembered what?"

"I remembered I gotta go."

"Go where? We are going to Estel's."

"I gotta date."

"You got a date."

I could have made scratch lasagna during their exchange.

"Sit down. A date," Ronny chuckled. "Hi, Peggy," he smiled. "You going to stand there or come all the way in?"

Vinny walked into the kitchen, opened the fridge, and brought Peggy a beer. I wished I could have seen her face. Vinny held it in front of her.

"No thanks." She pushed it away with the back of her hand. "Would you excuse us?" She pointed a finger from Vinny to the door. "You gotta date, right?" she mocked.

Ronny stood up. "What the fuck. Vinny, just wait by the bikes."

Vinny took Peggy's beer along.

"Okay," Ronny sighed, "what's up? Don't tell me—the truck."

With the crime now stated, she said slowly, "Oh, you're goddamn right it's the truck." She took a step at him. "You rented a truck and made me believe it was mine. Fool me once, shame on you. Fool me twice—"

"Only twice?"

I got up and leaned against the railing to watch. I didn't want them to break anything.

"I never told you it was yours. I simply asked, how do you like this truck?"

"All right," Peggy held up both hands and turned away from him. She looked at me for half a second, and then rolled her eyes to the ceiling. She turned to face him.

"You wait until I see your nurse," she pointed. "I don't know what she believes about my daughter, but she hasn't heard from the daughter's mother. And you can bet your sweet ass she's going to."

"Go ahead," Ronny sat back on the couch. He took a long drink of beer, finished it, and crinkled the can. "I don't give a shit what you tell her. Labor Day's in one week."

"That's right," Peggy feigned surprise. "I plum forgot! Little Nurse Nightingale goes back up north, and the beaches close."

"My unemployment application is already completed."

Something about the way Peggy looked down from the ceiling and tensed her shoulders sent a chill up my back. "Fucker!" she screamed.

She took a couple of quick steps toward the couch, and I opened the slider. She stopped at the end of my radio table where she reached down and picked up my 1964 World's Fair ashtray and cocked it behind her ear.

"No," I ran in, "no, no, no."

She didn't lower the ashtray. It vibrated in her hand. Eyes flaring, chest heaving up and down, she stood like that until I came around in front of her.

"Easy now."

I reached up with my free hand and took hold of the astray. She gripped it tighter. I took her wrist and tried to ease the ashtray down.

Ronny grabbed a pillow and held it in front of his chest. "Is that a minuet?"

"Fucker," Peggy hissed.

Linda opened the spare room door. "Mom, knock it off," she came over to us. She put her hands on her hips and stood right in front of her mother.

Peggy let go of my ashtray. She dropped her arm. "Goddamn you," she pointed at Ronny. She looked from Linda to Ronny. "There is no way you are getting away with this."

"With what?" Ronny smiled. He spread his arms, palms up, and then stood from the couch.

"Adults," I moved in front of Ronny. "Take this somewhere else."

"She called me," Peggy pointed at Linda.

"Conspiracy!"

"Shut up! Shut him up, Jimmy," Peggy tried to get past me.

In a back-asswards rugby scrum, I took Ronny's arm, pulled him toward my door, and slammed it. I put my shoulder to it so Peggy couldn't open it. I stood there catching my breath. I felt tired. After I was sure Ronny was long gone, I walked to the couch and sat. Linda sat next to me; Peggy stood in front of me. After five minutes of telling them I regretted all of it, I got up and ushered them toward the door. They both stopped.

"You go, Mom. Take my bike."

"Yes, ma'am."

Going down the stairs, Peggy laughed as if she'd spotted a butcher knife. I held Linda's arm tight above the elbow. She wasn't going anywhere just yet.

"Come on the balcony with me."

We caught sight of Peggy riding down Ocean Ave. She either wanted to catch Ronny or she remembered she had a cake in the oven.

"That bike's just too small for Margaret," Linda chuckled.

"She's your mother."

Linda fired up a cigarette. She knew I didn't let her smoke at my place.

"It was a bad idea to call her. I shouldn't have let you."

Linda snapped her head around. "You didn't know 'till after. And you laughed yourself sick. Hypocrite."

I'd taken a glass of water with me out on the balcony. I took a good long drink and then put the glass down on a tray table. "You're right."

"I'm sorry. I shouldn't have said that."

"It's okay."

She puffed on that cigarette as if it gave her something besides nicotine. Inhale, exhale. Lips popped apart to suck in, made a circle to blow out. On the last exhale, the filter bent against the railing top, ash dropping to the ground. She turned to leave.

"You didn't tell me."

"Tell you what?"

"Whether you want Tuesday morning or Tuesday afternoon."

"Oh, she sighed, "can I tell you tomorrow?"

"Sure."

I picked up the water. It felt cold going down. Too cold—freezing. Like ice cream. Then I remembered. "I start all the way down south tomorrow."

"Okay." She left. I looked for her. I didn't see her, so I leaned forward. She stepped from under the balcony.

"Gotcha," she smiled up. She started toward the boards. "I still say it was hilarious," she called back.

Hours later, a fist pounded on my door. It jarred me awake. I reached for my voice. The overhead light flicked bright. I walked to the door, turned the lock, and half pissed-off, opened the door.

Ronny stood in my doorway. He had a red bandana around his head. Underneath the bandana a fat wad of white gauze stuck above one ear. He looked like a bandaged sewer rat—hair and clothes dripping wet.

"Want to hear what happened?" he smiled.

"Looks like it's raining." I showed him in and locked the door behind him. "This better be good." I walked back to my room and climbed in bed. I propped an elbow—rested my head. "Let's hear it."

He came into my bedroom slowly. He stood there staring at me.

"Sit down, for chrissakes," I held a hand out at the foot of the bed. Then I smiled. "Just like Vinny with his sweats. It's okay. You won't catch anything off my covers."

"What about your last partner?" His smile held no malice.

"Perfectly healthy. I know him like the palm of my hand."

He sat down, laughed, and then touched his hand to where the gauze stuck out from under the bandana. He winced, "Here goes."

15

LOCH ARBOUR PAULIE, the tsunami-haired ab freak, always wanted to be a male model. His place was a photo-shoot shrine. The walls were covered with poster-size shots—close-up Paulie, Brooks Brothers Paulie, Karate Gi Paulie. Some modeling agents in north Jersey had called him to come up for a photo shoot. Thrilled out of his rowing shorts, Paulie phoned Darlene and quit his job.

The plan was to get together at Estel's for Paulie's sendoff.

Ronny fled warpath Peggy with every intention of making it to Estel's in time for Paulie's arrival. He didn't make it. On her too-small bicycle, she pulled up to Estel's before he stepped past Tony Stallion at the front door.

"I'm on my way to Sussex between A and B Street," she screamed. "A little cottage with a scalloped awning fringe around the porch. Know it?"

Last week of August—too late to apologize—it wouldn't serve a purpose. He came down Estel's stairs and for once told the truth.

"Look Peggy don't screw this up for me. It's been a long summer. I really like Robin, and I want to be with her."

"Well, now that's touching," Peggy stretched down her feet off the pedals. "What about my truck?"

"The truck. It's in the Hertz lot."

"I want that truck back, fucker. That or another one."

He didn't know what else to do. "Let's go in and have a beer."

"That's not happening." She pulled a crumpled pack of cigarettes from her shorts' pocket, took one out, and lit it. It was split in the middle. She held it out and watched the smoke curl from the break. "Everything happens to me on goddamn Sunday." She bent the cigarette straight and tried to take a drag. She held it up to her face. "This is what happens when you ride a kid's bicycle."

"Looks like it's had a long day."

Inside Estel's, the Begonias started up a new set. He looked up at the music. Through the big picture window heads bobbed up and down to the beat.

"All the boys are in there. Paulie got a model shoot. We're celebrating."

"Paulie? Who the hell's Paulie?"

"From Loch Arbour. The guard with black hair. He told me he thinks you're hot."

"Another kid."

"He's twenty-one."

"When you say you want to be with her, what do you mean? Always? As in marry?"

He reached for her hand holding the cigarette, pinched shut the break, and used it to light one of his own. "Try this one," he handed it to her. "I'm going in. You do what you have to do, what you want. I can't stop you."

Peggy looked down at the bike. "I can't leave this here. Somebody will take it." She looked around. "Where'd you put yours?"

He pointed to the Speed Limit 25 MPH sign. "You can share my lock."

She shook her head.

"Ride it home and come back. It's three blocks."

She looked at him. A sad smile crossed her face for a moment. Then she picked up the bike. "I'll walk it. The seat hurts my ass."

She seemed calmer. Probably stay home he thought. He waited until she turned west on Chester before heading for the noise and light that spilled out of Estel's. Jumping in line, he wormed his way past people by tapping the top of one hand with the other and repeating, "Been in, been stamped."

One guy said so what. Ronny looked back, smiled, and kept cutting. At the door, he winked at Tony Stallion and stepped inside. "Uncle John's Band" greeted him along with the L.A. crew—Vinny, Teddy, and Paulie, along with some Belmar boys. Faces turned and a beer came his way as he got a fist salute from the Begonia's lead singer.

"Where's Peggy?" Vinny laughed.

"Where's your date, asshole? You're scared of that woman, aren't you?"

"I keep seein' her with a knife."

"Here's Mr. JC fucking Penny."

"Hey, Cap'n," Paulie managed.

Ronny shook his head. "You're trashed. You watching out for the Belmar guard you sucker punched?"

"Can you watch? Shit, don't let him hit my face!"

"Watch out for Donaldson and that one friend of his," Ronny said into Vinny's ear.

"Gottcha."

The place was three beers ahead of him. That shit of Jimmy's kicked ass. "Play something fast!" he called to the band. Nope— "Fire on the Mountain." Everybody in the place moved in slow motion. He remembered this set— "I Know You Rider" was coming up. He'd fix this place.

It took him a long time to get there—the bar was four and five deep. Reaching over a short guy in front of him, he yelled, "I need a few shots of the mouthwash, Jerry. Start with ten." He turned, counting people, and didn't see Peggy come through the door. "Better make it twenty." He handed out eight shots in plastic cough medicine sized cups stuck between fingers on both hands. He missed Peggy snagging somebody's half-full Bud bottle off the picture window counter.

Back to the bar for round two—Ronny'd given shots to strangers to hold his place. Peggy was waiting for him. As he passed her, she whipped the Bud up from one hip and smacked it against his head.

The Begonias' lead singer saw it all. "China Cat Sunflower" turned into "Holy shit, lady!"

Half the bar stopped. Half kept right on. Peggy looked down at her hand. It held the bottle's neck. She opened her hand and watched it drop to the floor.

Hand on his head, Ronny straightened up and turned. He stared at Peggy. He shook fingers through his hair. Pieces of glass fell. His one hand came away bloody.

Tony Stallion and another bouncer were on it.

Ronny looked at Vinny. "Some fuckin' back-watcher you are."

"It wasn't Donaldson."

Peggy turned at Stallion, "Don't touch me!" She froze, held up both hands. Then with her head cocked at a point-made angle—stepped toward the door.

Blood ran past Ronny's ear and turned chin-ways down his cheek. Stallion brought bar towels. He tossed one to Ronny. He picked up the bottle neck, dropped a bar towel or three onto the floor, and stuck a foot over them to wipe up the blood and beer spots on the floor.

The Begonias plunked the first notes of "Shakedown Street." "Let the evening continue along its merry path," said the lead singer.

Holding a bar towel to his head, Ronny made for his bicycle. He told me his story later.

He wasn't about to waste such an opportunity. As he peddled along Ocean Ave, he kept raising a hand to his cheek. He didn't want a trail of gore running down his face when Robin opened the door. She'd told him she was staying in tonight. Have fun with Paulie and the boys. Every time his right foot came around to the bottom of a pump, his head throbbed.

The lights blazed in the little cottage on Sussex. Around the porch light bulb, moths and black beetle-things darted and bounced like bumper cars. He had no idea what the hell he was going to say if Lisa answered the door, looked at his head, and laughed serves you right.

He got Robin.

"Ronny, my God."

"I'm a mess, nurse."

"Stay right there. No, sit down. On that one," she pointed to a porch chair. "I'll be right back. Good," Robin popped open the screen door, "under the light. Right there."

When she came back out, she lifted his hand and the towel off his head. She stood in the porch's middle and slipped on latex gloves from a first aid kit she'd brought.

"Tilt your head down, please."

He sat, waiting for the questions. None came. She fussed with gauze and a pair of scissors from the first aid case. Her white shorts and bare legs stood right in front of him when he lifted his eyes.

"Can Lisa get me a beer while you're doing this?"

"Ron, shut up. Lisa's not home."

"You walk around me like Louie the barber used to when I was a kid getting a haircut. My mother would pick me up. She taught me to tip 20% and handed me a quarter to give to Louie. Not the owner, though."

"Who was it?"

"I forget. Oww, shit!"

"Hold still. I mean the name of the person who hit you—with a beer bottle, judging from the brown glass in your hair."

"Don't cut out a chunk."

"Of what?"

"Hair!"

She kept dabbing the wound with alcohol or disinfectant—something that burned like hell. A pile of crusty-blood cotton balls collected by his feet.

"Hate to tell you," Robin stepped back. "They need to shave the spot in the ER."

"Stitches?"

"Four or more, I'd say."

"I don't want to look," he said in her car after leaving the emergency room, "but I will anyway." He pulled down the sun visor—no light for the mirror. "I must look like the guy in the spirit of '76."

Robin smiled. "Sorry. It's an economy car. Once the gauze comes off, with your mop the spot won't be visible."

"Will I have to put Coppertone on it?"

"Wear a hat."

"No hats."

"You were so brave when Nurse Marilyn gave you the Novocain, shaved your little spot and sewed your stitches. Isn't that what you want to hear me say?" she laughed. "What's this place I'm looking for?"

"We're looking for a fresh-squeezed screwdriver. Take 35 south."

She drove over the 35 bridge and turned left into Belmar She found a diagonal space, parked, and together they walked toward Tessinger's.

"Think they'll let you in in that get up? A bloody sweatshirt and rowing shorts?"

"Blood shows up well on the orange sweatshirt. You'd think it wouldn't, but it does," he pulled at a sleeve.

They turned the heads of old geezers sitting at the bar, and one table filled by two couples took notice as they passed and found seats at the bar's end underneath the TVs. He recognized the bartender—the same one who worked the night he'd come in with Peggy and Jimmy. Gerry, his nameplate read.

"Just my luck," he muttered.

"What?"

He smiled extra wide when the bartender came over. "Hi, folks."

"Two screwdrivers please. Remember me?"

Gerry looked at Robin and smiled. "Does he want me to?"

"I don't know. He mumbles after head trauma."

Ronny turned to show Jerry his gauze. He pointed to it.

"Oh, I see now." Gerry made the screwdrivers and brought them. He nodded and looked at Ronny before taking the money. "Out of twenty."

"She's my nurse. She patched me up."

Gerry smiled at the register. He brought the change. He dropped silver and bills and counted, "Five, ten, and ten makes twenty. Enjoy."

Robin sipped through her straw. She always looked up at him when she sipped. It made him feel like they were kids on drugstore stools. He had the feeling that summer had been leading up to this moment. That all her nonsense had brought him here, on this stool, in this bar, with this girl.

"You didn't ask who hit me."

"I think I did."

"Peggy. She clocked me. I was here with her once. Jimmy was with us. Now you're going to ask why Peggy clocked me."

"I'd go easy on that drink. Alcohol's not the best thing to drink after you've had your head conked."

"Three stitches. Not as bad as you thought."

She swiveled around and faced the bar. She took one pretzel stick from the munchie bowl in front of them and nibbled on an end. In the baseball game on the TV above them, Phil Rizzuto yelled holy cow. Robin got off her stool, walked a few feet, and looked up.

"Well?"

"Out of here, home run! Holy cow!" she lifted her arms and turned to look at him.

"Who?"

"Wait—he's coming home. Number 31. Oh, he is a big, good-looking man."

"Dave Winfield."

She stood with her arms folded. She smiled at him. "You can stand all by yourself and come see."

Ronny kept his eyes on the TV. Henderson scored ahead of Big Dave. The two-run shot made it 5-2 Yanks. "They'll replay it."

"Too bad you can't do that in real life." She sat down next to him and touched his cheek with the backs of her fingers. "Head hurt?"

"Thanks for not lecturing."

"It's all up to you."

"No more replays. Except with you."

They sat and watched the game. They sipped the drinks. Two innings passed.

"Do you want to go?" she asked several times.

"I'm fine," he smiled each time.

Between innings she told him, "I like this place. Why haven't you brought me here?"

"It's dull."

She leaned close to him. "It's quiet. There's a difference. Does your head hurt?" She lowered her chin and smiled, "It will, you know. Once the Novocain wears off."

"Is that so?"

"Yes."

"No, it doesn't hurt. Let's go before the Novocain quits."

He left a five on the bar. A discreet bartender meant everything.

Before they reached her car, she said, "You should know about this Novocain business after your splinter."

He stopped, took her arm, held up his right foot, and hopping, pointed down at it. "It went clean through," he mocked the voice of Marilyn, the nurse in the ER who had stitched his wound. "From one side of the foot to the other."

"Please, let's go."

"So where did the bandana come from?" I smiled after he finished.

"Robin gave it to me. I guess to keep the gauze on. The wrap from the ER came off. You mind if I sleep here tonight? I'm beat. My head's playing a drum solo."

"Guest room's all set."

Ronny stood up. "Thanks. Thanks, Jimmy."

"Did you mean what you told Peggy?"

"About Robin? I meant it. I know you have no reason to believe me. Neither did Peggy."

"Does Robin?"

"She has the best reason. It's the same as mine."

16

ONE WEEK FROM Labor Day I spotted Linda riding on the boards. She peddled up the bike ramp and walked up to my gate. In a sundress with her hair pulled back from her face, she looked like a debutante riding a kid's bicycle. I'd never seen her wear real shoes before.

"I can help you tomorrow morning. It's going to be a good beach day."

I gave her the up and down look. "Awfully dressed up for a Monday. Priorities close to Labor Day? Do I know him?"

"Jimmy," she shook her head.

"Is he a school friend?"

She leaned her bike against the storm fence. "Don't even mention school."

"Does he have a name?"

She let her bike drop and put her hands on her hips. "You're going to keep at it, aren't you?"

"It's in my job description."

I had my voice at my side. I liked to mouth my words to Linda. She was the only person I felt comfortable speaking to directly. It was how we talked. Linda would lean toward me, shake that mane of hair, and for an end mark punctuate every sentence with a chewing-gum smile. I'd have my voice at my side. She could discern my one-breath, grumbled roar just fine.

We both laughed at my job description line—I always joked that giving her beer and cigarettes wasn't in my job description—just as a big SUV pulled into a space along the boardwalk. It was a brand-new vehicle—still had the sticker on the side window. I didn't recognize the driver because of the early morning glare coming off the windshield. Whoever it was stayed inside while Linda and I laughed. She came close in for a hug.

"I'm not telling you his name. You'll crack up."

I looked over Linda at that SUV. Out climbed my son-in-law. He walked to the parking meter, plunked in a quarter he'd had in his fist when he got out of the vehicle, checked his watch, and headed for the ramp steps. He wore dark slacks and a white, short-sleeved shirt with a red knit tie. He always dressed like the Michael J Fox character in *Family Ties*.

"Holy shit," I mouthed.

Linda turned to look.

I lifted my voice. "Bill." I watched him come. "Hello, Bill," I extended a hand, "what brings you—"

"Good morning," he held up a hand, his index finger waving. "I just stopped to tell you." He looked at Linda. "Would you excuse us, please?"

"Sure," she threw up both hands. "Sheesh."

He looked after her. When she sat on the second bench down from my gate, he turned to face me, and then looking back at Linda said, "Isn't that the girl who was with you a few weeks ago when we saw you?"

"Yes."

As hard to read as a billboard, his parochial brain twisted away putting one and one together to make five.

"So. Alice asked me to stop by before we go away today." He took a breath after the sentence almost the way I have to when I speak without my EL. "She says to tell you that we'd like to invite you to our place Labor Day for a picnic." He stared at me as if waiting for me to kiss his ring.

"That's great. You give Alice my love and have a great vacation. Where are you heading?"

"Cape May."

"Right. You two love it down there."

"We're taking the girls."

Shit. My underage girlfriend and I were planning to come by and molest them. "Of course you are." I stuck out my hand again. This time he took it, limp-wristed me a few times, and backed up.

"Have a good week."

"Bye-bye, Bill!" Linda called.

She waved a hand over her head. He boosted himself back up into his battleship.

Linda came over, and we watched him back out and swing an illegal Ocean Ave U-turn back south.

"Where are the cops when you want one?"

"Your Bill bought himself a new Explorer."

"It's from his dealership. He told me I could come to their picnic Labor Day."

"Actually, he said, 'We think it's fine if you visit.' Southeast breeze this morning."

She hopped on her bike. The streamers were gone. Shiny, dangling earrings glittered next to her cheeks.

"Tomorrow morning at my place. Wear jeans."

She started peddling. "It's Billy Harris!"

I should have guessed. Robin wasn't home when I called during my lunch break. Who would be inside on such a nice day?

Same story after I got off. I called her from home and got no answer. Waiting to try once more, I listened to rumbles of thunder and watched a quick shower. When I called again, her phone echoed like a dirge. On a Monday, where else could she be?

Summer sounds that came to me on my balcony that evening: the empty, repetitive ring of a phone, car tires passing on a wet street, a train whistling in the distance, the dinging of the Inlet Bridge as its gates choked the flow of Ocean Ave traffic.

In the quiet, I pictured scenes from earlier in the season: dancing at Estel's, trudging happily to find lost parking spots, holding my wallet tight as bouncers dragged me from the Gull's Room at the Tropical, standing in a summer bar line anticipating seeing Ronny and Robin.

As I smiled, remembering, I saw my former self in those lines from summers past, announcing my presence with a booming voice instead of a mechanical whisper. I could join in the chorus of catcalls and whistles. I could look at myself in men's room mirrors and never admit who I was, who I loved, who I mistreated. In fear of being discovered, I buried myself in my anger. I stood in line to disappear.

Now I stood in line to belong. I called again. Robin answered as if she'd just run up three flights of stairs.

"Hello. Were you jogging?"

"Jimmy, no. No, I just came from Shop-Rite. Unloading stuff." In the background female voices lifted and vanished.

"Are you throwing a party?"

"We all went together—the whole house. Stop it—it's Jimmy." She covered the phone. "Sorry," she came back. "At Shop-Rite some of us sipped wine from our Pepsi cups."

I waited to speak. I had a grin on my face.

"Jimmy?"

"Right here. What's the story for tomorrow?"

"What time do you want me? Is it going to be hot? I didn't see any weather today. It was beautiful today."

"At Loch Arbour?"

"Yes, at Loch Arbour."

"How's his head?"

"Oh, he's fine. He's a big baby. Three stitches—he told me he told you. Thanks for putting him up last night. Jimmy, that woman's insane. She should be locked up."

"No comment. Listen, I know it's asking a lot, but how about the afternoon? I have Linda helping me in the morning. We'll do the digging, and you and I can do the planting."

"Okay, in the afternoon." What a racket. I pictured them all in that tiny kitchen.

"I said stop it!" she laughed.

I pictured the white and blue striped lighthouses on the top half of the back door curtains.

"Any time after noon. Okay?"

"Okay. Bye, Jimmy."

"Goodbye," I said after she hung up.

That evening, I hit Hallow Bros. Nursery on 35. I'd called ahead with my order, and they had it all set to go. Thank goodness I had the Caddy. A convertible is almost as good as a truck.

Tools, bagged mulch, plants, blood and bone meal, peat moss—altogether it cost me damn near $250.00. So much for my estimate. With the Caddy's trunk packed full of bags and tools, the back and half the front seats covered with plant materiel, I turned off 35 to stop at Tessinger's.

Gerry tended the bar. I sat at the end by the newspapers so I could look out the windows to keep an eye on my car. It was almost dark. The day's last light filtered through the blinds. Gerry came over and greeted me.

"Expecting somebody out there?"

"I have a Chamaecyparis in my backseat."

Gerry's smile never waned. He'd bartended long enough to know when to let things pass.

One cold draft Rheingold," I ordered.

"That it?"

"I have to perform physical labor tomorrow."

"That's a good thing."

"A damn good thing."

He drew the beer into the tilted pilsner glass before lowering it to let the head form. He took away the glass after cutting the tap. The foam spilled up over the edge. He smoothed it with a head cutter. Then he plucked a coaster off the top of the stack, spun it onto the bar in front of me, and set the glass down bull's-eye. That beer went down in a hurry. "Maybe one more, Gerry, and give it a peat-flavored friend in a wee glass."

17

RIGHT ON TIME next morning, Linda's pig tails reminded me of Dorothy from The Wizard of Oz. Except the fluffed hair on her forehead still lifted like a wave set to break. She wore a T-shirt and cutoff jeans. She dropped her bike on the grass and looked up at me on the balcony with her hand up to shield her eyes.

"How's this for punctuality?"

"Good word. Nice cutoffs."

"I look like a hippie from the Sixties."

"I'll meet you there. There's no room for your bike."

"You're going to make me ride to and from Sea Girt?" She stood with her hands apart, gaping as if I'd just shot her.

"It's you or the plants."

We took turns with the garden spade digging the bed's new outline. I stretched a hose in the rough curve I wanted. Linda put the spade precisely against the hose when it was her turn to dig.

"We don't have to be exact."

"Why are we using a straight shovel to dig a curved line?"

"You'll see."

I'd told her no flip-flops—she'd worn sneakers. "It still hurts my arches when I push the spade into the ground."

"Stop stomping down."

We finished the outline before she whined me to death. I told her to ride into Sea Girt to get a soda while I cut the back edge of the bed. I had most of the rectangular pieces of sod turned up by the time she returned. We stacked the sod clumps around back.

122

"Bill can cover his roof with them if there's ever a forest fire."

Linda didn't find that as funny as the splotches of dirt on my face. I kept wiping sweat with a bandana and got the clean side mixed up with the dirty.

We unloaded the Caddy, placed the plants, and stepped back to the street.

"When it comes to the perennials, you have to picture at least three years down the road," I explained. "More for shrubs."

"Why?"

"Spread and growth."

Linda really had a great eye. She saw things I missed. For instance, she foresaw that I had the coneflowers too close to the Chamaecyparis. We both dug around the landscape ties. Half of them pulled right out in rotten pieces. I loaded them in my trunk on top of the tarp I'd brought. She had one curlicue of hair that kept falling over her right eye. Every time it dipped, she puckered her mouth at the corner and blew the hair back up.

After she helped me amend the bed with the blood and bone meal, I told her she could call it a morning. It was about eleven-thirty.

"Here you go," I handed her fifty dollars, all in tens. "You save that for something. Don't spend it on cigarettes."

"Wow! Uncle Jimmy!"

"Better than union wage."

After she left, I was so damn hot and tired, I sat in the Caddy's AC for about ten minutes before I drove off for home. I had two cups of coffee for lunch. My fingers quivered when they weren't around my mug.

At one o'clock, I locked the place up and headed south back to Alice's birthday present. Robin's car was parked right out front. She was bent over, digging in the bed with a hand trowel. She really did have a cute butt. I wasn't too tired to notice that.

"Hey," she straightened up and turned. She wore garden gloves. A head band held her hair up on top of her head like a snowdrift.

I walked closer to speak. "That where a gaillardia's going to live?"

"I thought I'd warm up with the holes for the #1 pots."

I pointed to the wheelbarrow. "That's the amended fill. It's all set to go."

"Was Linda with you this morning?"

"She did great. A very good worker."

She turned and finished digging. She had all the holes for the perennials done. I saw a thin line of sweat run down her cheek as she stepped back onto the lawn. "I saved the evergreen holes for you," she smiled.

I picked up the shovel. She put a hand above mine as if we were kids gripping up a bat to see who hit first.

"Jimmy, I'm kidding. You plant the plants. I'll take care of the holes."

She took the shovel slowly as I let my hand come away. When she started in on the hole for the Chamaecyparis, I uttered a quiet thank you. I felt as if I'd run a marathon in the soft sand next to the boards.

We left Bill's midget sentry spruces in. They'd look more ridiculous—if they could be seen at all—as the perennials filled in. For an immediate improvement, the blue star junipers bordering the Chamaecyparis looked striking. As for that corner yew, I sawed off that bastard at soil level. It didn't deserve the effort to dig out its roots.

We stood in the street and paced up and down in front of the house after we finished. The John Deere tractor lady stuck her head out and back in her doorway turtle-style.

Robin nodded in her direction, "Is that the neighborhood watch?"

"The first time that woman saw me she thought my voice was a gun."

We were both sweating, wiping our faces. I went to the Caddy and pulled two ice-cold Buds out of my cooler.

"They've been marinating in ice water for hours."

"Thanks, Jimmy," she held up a hand. "I still have errands to run. What I need is a long, cool shower."

"I don't have a key for Alice's house, or I could let you in."

"Oh, no."

I ended up drinking both Buds before Robin left. She told me about a dozen times how nice the plants looked and what a lovely birthday surprise for Alice when she came home from Cape May. We said our good-byes. I almost asked what she was doing for the weekend.

She had her car door open when I remembered about Labor Day. "Hey, I forgot to tell you. Alice invited me over for a Labor Day picnic."

"Oh, Jimmy, that's great! You'll get to visit your granddaughters."

"Bill came to see me. Can you believe it?"

"Excellent," she climbed into her seat.

In the moment before her car started, I remembered kissing her at Lughnasa. I could picture it. I kissed her forehead and let my lips brush the feathers of her eyelashes before pausing on her cheek.

That's what two quick beers can do to me. I can remember names, dates, events—they all come back from somewhere after two beers or one stiff drink. Someone could make a trunkful of money if he ever found a way to package my two-beer memory secret.

18

E VEN A MAYFLY can make plans. I had the rest of my week mapped out. Each day, up to and including Labor Day, I knew exactly what I'd be doing. After that, I figured I'd be like a blown-up balloon when it's let go—I'd fly somewhere in a hurry and end up where I ended up.

Wednesday after work I took care of business uptown. I saw my lawyer and tied together loose ends as the saying goes. It felt weird not having to give him cash to post my bail.

I stopped in to see Gerry one last time at Tessinger's before I took a drive out to Tinton Falls to visit Mother and Father. It had been a while. I had to visit the lady in the office to get directions to locate their graves. I remembered that night at the dinner table in our old house when my father talked about the spaces he bought. Even though they weren't all together, he'd bought enough for all of us.

Thursday, I worked my favorite Belmar blocks—from the Lake Pavilion down to Inlet. Annie didn't leave during her break. She stayed and visited with me. She was near the finish line of her latest cross-stitch creation.

"What are people like on Labor Day? Same as Memorial Day and the Fourth?"

"Oh, my," she laughed. "You haven't seen anything until you've worked Labor Day weekend."

"No? How come?"

She tucked her cross-stitch into the fold of her denim skirt the way she does when she gets serious about making a point.

"Jimmy, some people enjoy pushing. They aren't happy unless time's short, tempers flare, or there's a rush on. They're so set on having the best time they've ever had; they forget to relax. By Labor Day, they're all pushed out."

"How's that different from the Fourth let's say?"

"My theory is there's nothing to celebrate. No fireworks or parades. It's three days at the end of summer. Back to reality."

"Our school days never leave us."

She leaned forward and touched my forearm. "You're exactly right. The child in us always cries at the end of summer."

We sat together in our small gate guard area like brother and sister. At five o'clock as we packed up, I asked her.

"How about having a beer with me, Annie?"

She looked at me as if I'd just asked her what time the balloon goes up.

"A glass of wine then. I'll drive. We'll go up to Johnny's on 35. Maybe split a Turkey Sligo if we get hungry."

"A what?" she laughed.

"A Turkey Sligo. It's a sandwich."

We stood facing each other in our tight, little space. She gave me a look that reminded me of Sophie when we first started going out. Her eyes moved up from my chest to my face as her face turned upward and she smiled. "That sounds terrific."

Johnny's is sacred ground to many people. Irish themed, the place even gives out a supply of green yarmulkes on St. Pat's. Families go there after Sunday mass for brunch, and husbands stay all day long to watch football. The food is good; portions satisfy the heartiest eater, and the bartenders always say before they put a hand over the phone, "I'll look for him. Hold on."

The horseshoe bar had plenty of space on a Thursday evening.

Annie ordered two draft Buds and pulled out a barstool before I could ask her table or bar?

"You're a regular here?"

"Don't be silly. I haven't sat at a bar in years. My husband didn't approve of ladies sitting at a bar, escorted or not," she laughed.

I lifted my glass. "Here's to our partnership."

"Are we running away? I'll have to phone my mother up there," she pointed at the ceiling.

"If I supply all the materials, how long would it take you to sew a name and date on a quilt?"

"A name and date?"

"On a quilt. I have the quilt and material to make the letters. I just need somebody to do the work." I took out my wad of twenties and fanned them. "Name your fee."

"Jimmy Hanlon," Annie blushed and waved a hand back and forth at the money. "You'll have people thinking I'm a hooker."

"A hooker?" I smiled. The word sounded funny coming from Annie's mouth. "I'm serious. It wouldn't have to be done until the end of September. The quilt's already fancy, and I'll cut the letters and numbers."

"Well, if that's all." Annie took a sip of beer as if the glass's rim were dirty. "I can see to that, no trouble. That's just a matter of sewing. That's no great chore."

Annie told me she wasn't hungry until a guy at the bar across from us bought himself—you guessed it—a Turkey Sligo. I ordered one to go.

"I'll buy the Sligo. We'll split it."

"Good Lord," Annie leaned in to whisper, "I don't think I can finish half of that."

"We can get a small salad instead of fries."

"How are we going to split a salad?" She giggled on the word salad.

I grabbed a cocktail napkin and borrowed a pen from the bartender. Some of my best ideas end up on cocktail napkins, although cardboard coasters last longer.

I wrote while I spoke. I needed another hand. Annie held the napkin in place.

"I have the name and dates—May 23, 1970-July 31, 1987, Antony Paul Silva. I cut block letters for Antony's name and the months. I bought plastic numbers and traced them for the dates. I've got everything in my car to give to you."

It never occurred to me that Annie would finish the quilt by Labor Day. She must have worked every night after work until who knows what hour to get it done. Whenever I start thinking that people in general are varying degrees of assholes, I think of Annie. What a sweetheart.

After I dropped off Annie, I visited Denny. He has a house on Barclay and C Street that his mother owned before she moved into a smaller place. I peeked in through the door curtain. Denny sat on the sofa eating from a tray table. It made me sad to see him. Day after day at dinner time, he probably sat alone in the same damn spot with a different sandwich.

I stayed about half an hour. We had a nice chat, small talk, before I got around to my visit's purpose. I asked him if he knew anything about the A.I.D.S. Names Project.

"The what?"

"On October 11th in Washington, quilts with the names of A.I.D.S victims are going to be spread on the mall."

"I never heard of it."

"I didn't know if you had any friends, any friends you've lost."

"I don't go anywhere, Seamus. You know that. I work and keep an eye on Mom."

"This gate lady I know is making a quilt. You know Annie down on Inlet?"

"Sure, Annie Collier. She lives on Locust."

"She'll have the quilt all done by the end of September. It's all paid for. You pick it up and hang onto it. Then take it to D.C. Maybe you and a friend can go together. It's supposed to be a big deal."

He shook his head no. "I don't know. A.I.D.S. scares the hell out of me, Seamus. So you know somebody who died of it?"

"It scares the hell out of everybody. That's why people who get it get blamed. Look," I told him, "this town lost a boy this summer, the boy who drove into the Inlet, remember? He died because of silence. That's A.I.D.S.'s accomplice right now—silence."

Denny didn't know what to say. It seemed to me like the best way to get Antony Silva's name in the record book. I wanted everyone complicit or innocent that morning to remember Antony. I wanted his name read out loud. That was the plan for October 11th.

"In the end, Denny, you might want to do it for yourself, quilt, or no quilt. I mean take the drive down there." I stood up.

"Why don't we go together?"

I turned and looked into his blue eyes. "I won't be around, my friend. I'm taking a trip. October 11th. It's a Sunday," I gave him a hug.

He saw me out. "I'll think about it."

19

ANYTHING IS POSSIBLE on 5-for-$1 night at Ray's.

By midnight it's a subway car at rush hour filled with drunks. They pack in; they swarm. Someone might materialize next to you, snatch a pony glass right out of your hand, and laugh in your face. He might walk past a gorgeous girl in a tube top, gently wet kiss the delicate curve of her neck where it trails down to bare shoulder, and then watch with a wry smile as she overreacts, screams obscenities, and gets escorted out of the door by two bouncers. He might smile at you, make conversation, and at the same time piss on your foot.

I've watched Ronny do all those things.

I wanted to see him and speak to him. I'd let his story from the other night sink in.

I parked the Caddy along the boards down by Albright. A space one block away was damn lucky to find even if I did beat the rush. It was before dusk. Twilight painted clouds over the water purple and pink. Traffic along Ocean Ave moved right along with not a bit of hurry. I wasn't feeling like a big beer night. My half Turkey Sligo filled up my gut like a wet roll of toilet paper. The walk from the Caddy didn't help.

I ordered a shot of peppermint schnapps to get the digestion juices moving as the crowd started to file into Ray's. Soon the bar space and bar stools were full. One bartender stood at the taps and filled ponies while the others delivered. One guy with long, thick arms cradled ten or so ponies with a forearm and hand, brought the other arm up tight against the glasses, and carried the whole bunch down the bar without spilling a drop.

I wasn't expecting the L.A. crew much before nine, nine-thirty. Girls never showed up before ten. They usually came in packs, attractive and confident. These were city girls, brash enough to handle themselves in cute little shore bars like Ray's. I liked the way they took care of each other. Even later, I could picture the place full of Labor Day head-starters down from up north. All they had to do was take off Friday. Why not?

I blinked, and it was three-deep behind me. That was reason number two for drinking schnapps—if I got up to pee, there was no way I'd have a stool when I got back. All the bartenders in Ray's were kids—a lot of them Belmar guards—that I didn't know. I felt like an old stone lion without its mate on a front porch.

Right after I threw back shot number three—I nursed the first two—I spotted Ronny with Paulie, Vinny, and Robin. I shook my head wondering what the hell she was doing in this place. She had on a slim, white cotton sundress with a modest neckline and sleeves that just covered her shoulders. Between the colored lights and white dress, she looked as tan as a walnut.

The four of them made their way to the end of the bar. People shied away from there because it was a narrow space bordered by a wall—tough to slide out to the dance floor or pee. Speakers thump-thumped away like a goddamn jackhammer. The lights over the dance floor down the way pulsed as the first brave souls ventured underneath the blinking spots.

Soon the small rectangle was surrounded by standing, swaying bodies. Pocketbooks lay on the dance floor edge. At each corner a folded-arm giant kept watch. Nobody and I mean nobody messed with dance floor bouncers. Those pocketbooks were as safe as Fort Knox. Hell, the owner would kill the thief before the bouncers could save him.

I didn't feel good. I figured one last pop before heading over to Robin and the boys. I got a shot after I don't know how long. For some reason, I tried talking to the bartender to tell him I was moving. I pointed down the bar to show him where. Head shaking no, he pursed his lips, pointed to his ear, and scooped up my change.

I wiggled out of my stool, stood up, and looked back down the bar. Everybody had disappeared—no Robin or Ronny in sight. Standing there, I searched for them between bobbing heads. I know I looked all around. My bar seat gone, my breathing getting raspy in all that smoky, sweaty air, I headed for an exit.

Outside on a picnic table seat, I gathered myself. I didn't know if it had been the heat, noise, or schnapps—but something had my head spinning. Auras circled headlights along Ocean Ave. Voices from passersby and the crowd standing in line to get into Ray's sounded far away.

I crossed the street and sat on a bench facing the ocean. The voices eased up there; even the traffic seemed to find a rhythm. I took deep breaths—felt the breeze cool the sweat on my forehead. I closed my eyes for what seemed like a short time. Then I felt a hand on my shoulder.

I opened my eyes and saw faces looking down at me as if I was fucking Rip Van Winkle waking up. Faces with no torsos, just straight arms with hands on knees.

"Jimmy," a female voice said. Fingers tapped my cheek.

"Hey! Wake the fuck up!" That was Ronny. "The cops don't like boardwalk sleepers."

He and Robin straightened me on the bench and sat on either side of me.

"Are you okay?"

I smiled at her. "I'm fine. I dozed off."

"We saw you leave an hour ago."

"It wasn't an hour."

"It was a while ago."

"Miss Timex," Ronny pointed.

I took my bandana out of my pocket and cleared my stoma. I felt okay— stiff, and my ass hurt—but okay. I looked at Robin. Her dress looked as if she'd been squirted in a water pistol fight.

"What happened to you?" I laughed.

"Same thing that happened to him," she leaned forward, smiling at Ronny, "except I won."

"We were asked to leave." Ronny's shirt clung in wet folds to his chest. His jeans looked as if he'd pissed himself. Wet hair plastered his forehead. "Damn," he shivered, "it's cold out here, Doc." He touched palms together. "Cold and sticky."

"Be patient, Patient. Let's be sure about this guy," Robin patted my leg.

"She calls you Patient?"

"Just then."

"Well, I'm fine. Tell me all about this." I moved my hand up and down in front of her. "You were asked to leave? It's something to get kicked out of Ray's."

"We had a beer fight."

"That dreck is not beer. It's tepid suds with a disinfectant chaser. It's worse than piss."

"We made rules. No throwing—just spitting. In a stream," Robin puckered her lips, placed two fingers on either side, and pinched the pucker. "Like that."

"We practiced at the beach today with water. It was hot. Her idea," Ronny aimed a finger.

Robin looked down at herself and tugged away her dress.

"C'mon. Let's go get us a hot shower. Up, Jimmy. Up we go."

I got up. "I'm fine. I don't do this as nice if I'm doing it for cops." I smiled at her and spread my arms apart. She hugged me.

"You drove, didn't you?"

"I'm parked right down across from Albright."

They insisted on walking me down to the Caddy. I didn't argue. The walk sobered me right up. It was a walk I took knowing something important had happened. I knew exactly where we three had been, and I knew I'd never in a thousand years be able to replicate the emotions I felt whizzing around inside near the end of my summer journey.

As I stepped up my stairs, I heard the phone ring inside. I hurried unlocking the door and dropped my damn keys. I picked up on the fifth ring.

"Hello."

"Dad, hi. Did I wake you?"

"No, hell no. Are you back?"

"I've been calling. Were you out?"

"Yup. So you're back, right? It's Thursday. Of course you're back. Happy birthday, honey."

"Dad, the plantings are wonderful. I loved your card and note."

"I'm glad you like them."

"I used the little map you drew to show Bill what's what. He got out the Britannica to see what everything would look like. Dad, it's really nice. I love it."

"Well good."

"Did you do all the work yourself? My God, how long did it take you?"

"No, no. I had some helpers. Listen, that corner yew we took. The thing should have worn a uniform like those British guys outside Buckingham Palace."

Alice laughed, "It's okay."

"He's listening to you."

"No, he's out, down at the dealership. Something about August inventory problems."

"You sound down yourself."

"I'm not down."

"You just sounded a little down when you said no, he's out. Like you were sighing."

"Nope. Dad?"

"Right here. Alice, I've been meaning to call. We haven't talked about that time on the boardwalk."

"I know."

"Now you sound angry."

"Dad, please. I'm not angry. Stop reading into my words."

"Okay, okay. Sorry. Reading words hereby stopped."

"Reading into my words. Where did you go out tonight?"

"Actually, I went to Ray's. I met some friends."

"That's a pretty young crowd, isn't it? I mean in Ray's?"

"I also went out with Annie if that makes you feel better. We went to Johnny's and split a Turkey Sligo."

"Annie from your party?"

"Yup."

"She's very nice. How much did you have to drink tonight, Dad?"

"Not so much. I'm just in a good mood. I was in a good mood when you called, and now I'm in an even better mood."

"I just worry, that's all."

"You don't need to worry. I don't want you to worry. Listen, I want to talk about what I said on the boardwalk."

"Dad, I'm tired. We had a long drive today. The girls fidgeted the whole time on the Parkway."

"It won't take a minute."

"That reminds me. Are you coming to our picnic?"

"Sure. Absoblumin' lutely."

"Dad, Mom and maybe Stan are coming for the weekend. I didn't tell you."

Stan is Sophie's husband. "So? Are they staying for the picnic?"

"I think so."

"I haven't seen your mother for twenty-some years. That's fine. I'll be there for sure."

"Okay," her voice rose, "I didn't know."

"Now you know. How about that minute now?"

"Dad."

"Alice, you've had weeks to think about what I said. Why did you send your husband to invite me to your home? You're a big girl, and you're going to listen to me for one minute."

I waited for her to say something. All I could see was the look on her face that day on the boardwalk, as if the sun dipped into the Atlantic Ocean and popped back out. Sure, she'd brightened up when she left. Anybody can do that if you know you can jog away from the situation.

"Alice?"

"Dad, it doesn't matter. Why are you talking like that? What can you say in one minute?"

"Probably not enough."

"It doesn't matter, Dad. It doesn't change anything. Get it out of your head that you have to explain anything to me."

"Okay."

"You're right, I'm a big girl. You were a man before I was born. Please forget all this big speech talk, okay? I didn't need weeks to come up with that."

"I meant to call or visit."

"I've been calling, if you want to know. You're not easy to get ahold of. You need an answering machine."

"I'd have to make a recording. Imagine what a wrong number would think."

"As far as sending Bill, no one sent him. We wanted to let you know we were leaving, that's all."

"You're something else."

"And you need to stay the hell out of Ray's for God's sake."

I heard the smile. "I'll never set foot in the place again. See you Monday."

"Okay, great. Thank you again for the plantings."

"Happy birthday, honey. Hey, does Stan still chew with his mouth open like he did twenty years ago?"

"Good night, Dad. Love you."

"I love you too, honey. I'll see you Monday after my shift."

20

FRIDAY WAS A good day for ducks.

Thunder woke me up about three a.m. My pillow felt like a sponge—my sheets were soaked, too. I toddled out to the living room to check the thermostat. The AC was on. I opened the slider. The air blew damp and cool, so I kept the door open.

I rifled around the TV channels a few times before I found a decent movie—Humphrey Bogart and Lauren Bacall in *The Big Sleep*. I tuned in just in time to see my favorite movie punch. Bogie thumbs his coat's lapel just before he throws a beautiful straight right hand—no wind-up at all—to knock out a bad guy.

I watched until the end. The last shot after the action's all done is of an ashtray with two burning cigarettes—non-filters, of course. It reminded me of the ashtray in my living room that morning after Ronny and Linda packed her bike in the Caddy and took off.

I suppose if I considered the negative events of the summer, most of them started with that night. I never asked myself what if I'd opened my bedroom door and told Linda to get the hell home. That would do as much good as yelling to warn the movie guy Bogie cold-cocked.

I knew one thing. As an adult, Ronny had been the ultimate rover. What scared him to death was being still. I figured maybe he'd hit that settling down period in Harris' textbook we laughed about on the Inlet guard stand back in June. He had a new anchor in Robin. I could think of one more—a place to call home. If I could get Ronny to take over my condo's mortgage at a bargain price, we could both profit. He understood the word profit just fine.

I beat every living thing to Loch Arbour that morning but the gulls.

They hovered, circled, and landed wings spread, feet peddling, near an island of litter. Near the tipped guard stand, night partiers had left a collection of beer bottles and chicken bones courtesy of Colonel Sanders. He grinned upside down from his bucket as a big gull pecked at the remnants of a drumstick.

Out over the water, gulls flew in fractured columns behind an early charter fisher close to shore. Watched by their grounded mates, their cries hidden and then audible in the breaking waves, they seemed perfectly content to follow their prize.

My flip-flops left dry foot spots as I walked to the shoreline. High tide— shore break slid all the way up the tide rise. The rise looked steeper than the last time I'd visited. Down the beach, a wave broke in the cove—a wave that first rolled in another ocean pulled by our moon when it felt the tug of a solar system from a galaxy light years away.

The gray mist settled into a drizzle. I lifted my slicker's hood over my head and sat down after tucking my slicker's bottom under my ass so my shorts didn't get soaked. I fired up a bone, cupped my palm over it to keep the wet off, and watched the gulls. For all of their flying and swarming, they never played.

A rumble came to me from over the water. Dark clouds in straight lines stood motionless along the horizon. Overhead the clouds moved in layers, the dark and quicker blowing east underneath the lighter gray.

I felt a chill on my butt and pulled out my thermos. I'd filled it with hot coffee, a teaspoon of white sugar, a touch of whipped cream, and the John Jamison. What the hell did I care what Mrs. G smelled on my breath?

As far as I knew, I'd talk to Ronny and say goodbye to everyone all by eight-thirty. Then I'd beat it home and make it to work before nine. What were they going to do, fire me with three days left in the season for being a few minutes late?

I turned around when I heard a car door slam. It was Darlene. She parked in her spot in front of the office just as Mrs. G's car pulled into the lot and parked alongside. The office opened. Darlene lifted the plywood sheets and hooked them to the eyebolts on the ceiling. She only opened the north side boards that faced the entrance.

Not long afterward, locker boys started to arrive. They locked their bikes to the chain link fence by the lifeguard shack and strolled through the gate past Mrs. G. She handed out keys and said something to each one. The drizzle turned back to mist as if commanded by the start of the workday.

Labor Day—the last weekend to make tourist dollars, get laid, get tan, get serious or break up with him/her, swim at guarded beaches, dig toes in the sand, get ready for school, and wear white.

Last weekend you had to put up with a lot of crap: Bennys, traffic jams, seasonal rates, parking meters, cars blocking driveways, drunks pissing on hydrangeas, litter, one way streets, and frequent bridge openings.

Don't forget crazy divorcées, holier-than-thou sons-in-law, horny lifeguards, sophisticated teenage girls, bikes in a backseat, Bronx toadies with Cosmo girlfriends, dead boys in white Mustangs, voice machines, semen-smeared panties, ashtrays, phlegm, prejudice, hope, dreams, cancer, lies, lies, and more lies.

I walked up to the office. Her shirt, shorts and shoes all matching, Mrs. G welcomed me in a yellow dither.

"Oh, Jimmy," she put her hands on her cheeks. "I didn't put on my face yet. You're here early. Aren't you working today?"

"I'm here to see Ronny before I go to work."

"Ahh." She sounded as if I'd explained the meaning of life. "Excuse me." She snatched up her pocketbook and whirled out of the office, patting me twice on the shoulder on her way past.

"Off to her powder room," Darlene muttered. "Jimmy, I can't wait for this weekend to be over."

I smiled, "I know how you feel. What do you do in the fall?"

She dug through a drawer with receipts and rental forms. "I suppose I'll be back at Steinbeck's. At least until after the Christmas rush."

"So you'll stick to retail."

"Retail. The only thing I sell here, Jimmy, are lockers. I'm schooled in couture."

"You sold me."

"So what, you're here to see Ronny? It's such a crummy day."

"Just for a minute."

She laughed. "That's about as long as you'll get him away from his girlfriend."

"Girlfriend? Ronny has a girlfriend?"

"She's cute. Blue eyes, dirty blond hair cut like Dorothy Hamill, fluffy and bouncy. I think she's a nurse."

"I think I've seen her. Can I wait here for him?"

"Sure, wait anywhere. No sense getting wet. God, I hope it pours all weekend." She slammed the drawer shut. "I could burn all this down in a heartbeat. Don't tell Mrs. G I said that."

I put up a finger to shush my lips. "I'll wait in the lifeguard shack," I pointed a thumb.

The shack's plywood exterior looked more worn than I remembered. The door had a padlock set up that a locker boy had opened. Inside the place smelled like tanning butter mixed with gym locker. It looked the same as it had weeks before—same towels, T-shirts, and shorts hung on nails, same mirrors, the weights and bars, the couch and ax-chopped piss hole. I lit one of my anisette cigars to air out the place.

I didn't wait long. The Captain's voice echoed in the surf. I looked out and saw him standing at the office talking to Mrs. G. She had her matching yellow kerchief in place, and her cheeks looked rosier.

Ronny trudged toward the shack, his toes-first steps making little sand explosions. He lifted his eyes and smiled at me.

"Happy fuckin' Labor Day. I hope this rain picks up."

"I'm working rain or shine."

"Everybody works today." He squeezed past me and went inside. "Nice cigar."

"I thought it improved the smell. Is that hole for what I think it's for?"

"That's Vinny's work. On rainy days he smuggles beer in here. I told him I didn't care about the beer, but you can't let old lady G smell it on you when you go to the locker bathrooms. The next day he made himself a pee-hole."

"Ingenious."

"Vinny's great at anything that involves destruction of property."

"Sounds like someone I used to know."

"Used to, huh?" He cleaned off two nails to make room to hang his sweats and towel. "Some of this shit hasn't moved for weeks."

"You sound like you've had your fill of this place."

"Place and time." He looked at me. "I think I had it right back in June. This shit's getting old. I mean the guarding and everything that goes with it."

"You have lots of time. You know when I left my wife Sophie, I thought I'd stay away a few months and go back when I worked out a few things. I never worked them out."

He walked over to the deluxe couch, pushed a pile of clothes over, and sat down. "Like what? What didn't you work out?"

"Illusions, dreams. I had these illusions. After my father died, they sped around in my mind like a runaway train. All I could do was blow the hell out of the whistle. I flew past crossings and stops. I couldn't slow down. It took me a while to realize the damn train had derailed, and I had to climb onto a different train."

"It's been two years for me." His voice cracked on the words *for me*. He stood, walked across to the curling bar, and pumped away.

"Losing a parent marks our lives."

"You have an anniversary coming. Your surgery on Labor Day."

"Now that you mention it, I think it was a few days after Labor Day—I think the Wednesday after. I don't really remember."

"Kick-ass drugs probably."

"Yeah. The hospitals have great drugs. The adult version of having your tonsils out as a kid and getting all that ice cream."

He put down the curling bar. He looked different. Maybe it was just me. He stood and moved with a purpose in the middle of that disorganized shit hole. He gathered up a torp and set it in the line bucket. "I have to take this crap—"

"Hang on," I held up a hand and then checked my watch. "Place and time. I have a deal for you. My place is about $750 a month. If you cover three hundred of that, you can stay there while I go to Ireland. I'll throw in use of the Caddy for free."

He screwed up his mouth. "Ireland? What's in Ireland?"

"I'm going to look up some of the old folk's roots."

"When did you decide this?"

I looked at my watch again for effect. "I have to get to work. Three hundred a month. I'm letting my daughter know you're a caretaker."

"A caretaker?" he laughed. "What am I taking care of?"

"Me. Otherwise I can't afford the trip." It wasn't a lie.

He put down the line bucket and lit a cigarette. "It sounds good except for one thing."

I waited. I rolled my hand, nodding.

"I'm going to get more shit, that's all. Me taking over my gay friend's condo."

I laughed, "Who gives you shit?"

He laughed right back. "You'd be surprised. Let's just say I've had an interesting couple of weeks."

"That's how it works. Comments and whispers behind your back. Crowds swell on whispers."

"I never cared about what people said about me," he shook his head.

"Cared? Past tense? How's it feel on my side of the fence? Take my offer. Fuck those people. Think who you can have as a guest."

He smiled who, me? "I didn't miss that part. Match-making bastard." He came over to me with his hand outstretched. I took it, and we shook. "I'm sorry I ever—"

I cut him off. "Apologies should serve a purpose, you said once. I have an account all set up. Just pay the three hundred the first—"

"Business day of the month," he finished my sentence.

"Right." I loosened my grip on his hand and watched it, still open, slip slowly away. "I'll leave the keys in the mailbox and the paperwork by the radio." I walked over to the pee-hole and stuffed my cigar through. "Perfect ashtray for you—unbreakable." I headed for the door.

"You going to be around this weekend?"

I turned in the doorway. "I have an invite to my daughter's for a Labor Day picnic."

"Holy shit. I take it your son-in-law doesn't know your secret."

I looked him right in the eye. "Careful. You're whispering."

I'd taken about five steps on the beach when he called from the doorway, "I'll take good care of your place."

I spun around, backpedaling. "Tuesday night or after."

"Crazy old bastard. Have a Guinness for me."

"Not so old," I shook my head.

At the office Mrs. G said, "Jimmy, what is with this weather? I heard it was going to clear up this afternoon. It better for Labor Day weekend."

"Some things take time, Mrs. G—goodbye. Goodbye, Darlene."

Later, driving the Caddy to work, I laughed thinking about what I'd said to Mrs. G. The woman had no idea what the hell I meant about things taking time. She thought I meant the weather. She ran a beach club. Rainy days meant no guests, no money.

Mrs. G, bless her heart, didn't know drought. She had no idea how it felt to hear rumbles only to watch the clouds pass over without a drop, to walk on ground that stretched brown and parched, to endlessly wait until a thunderstorm boomed and poured buckets to wash everything clean, to break up a crowd and drown out the whispers.

21

MRS. G MUST have smiled. It cleared up just fine Friday. By the afternoon, a northeast breeze swept every cloud from the blue except for broom-stroke white icicles. The traffic along Ocean Ave swelled during the day. By quitting time, it barely crawled. I was able to jaywalk through the mess to save steps on my way to Ray's, where I wanted one cold beer before heading home. One cold, peaceful beer. Yes, I remembered what I'd told Alice.

I'd worked the south end of town, last stop Albright, and it was, after all, Labor Day weekend. The bouncer at the door swept me in like a volunteer fireman being a traffic cop—all arm wave and show.

Inside, the runners outnumbered customers. Buckets of ice and cases of beer zigzagged across the dance floor. Most of the bartenders—their white shirts with RAY'S identified them—sat around smoking cigarettes, drinking cups of coffee, and yakking to their mates. I felt like Claude Rains—could they see me?

I beckoned them—c'mon, c'mon. It's Labor Day, damnit.

One looked toward me, snuffed out his cigarette, and ignored me. Finally, he sidled over, still talking to his buddies.

"No, I'm not talking to her again. Jesus!" he called, his right ear facing me.

"Bottle of Dom Perignon and one glass, please."

"Say what?" he turned. He looked me up and down. I had socks his age.

"Hey, it's you," I wagged a finger at the son of a bitch. "I know your father."

"You know my father?"

"Nope. Keep looking. Bottle of Bud and a shot of peppermint schnapps."

144

I was surprised I got an actual shot glass. "Haven't stocked the Pepto plastic cups yet, hey?"

The bartender looked past me as a group of girls walked in. I finished my beer and headed for the Caddy. That morning, I'd parked her in a prime spot one block down. On Labor Day weekend, I felt like cruising topless. Besides, the AC had gone flat—it blew nothing but luke-warm.

Driving, more like crawling along Ocean Ave, I turned the radio up loud. I had a stashed pack of Pall Malls in the glove compartment, and I lit one. My thighs stuck to the hot leather seat. Sweat beads dripped down the back of my neck and laughed at the puffs of 5 mph stop-and-go air.

At the crosswalk on Seaside a whole tribe—and I mean a caravan of generations—left the boardwalk ramp. Two men led the way followed by women pushing baby carriages, kids walking bikes, older kids pulling wagons stacked with coolers and sand toys.

When two elderly couples at the parade's end made it between the white lines, the guy behind me lost it. He hit his horn twice. Five seconds later, he hit it again, this time one long blast followed by rhythmic pulses. He must have had a song in his head. Honk, honk, honk—like a goddamn hammer in my brain.

The two couples were past the Caddy's grill about halfway across when I opened my door and got out. First, I saw the orange and black license plate. Then the male driver and his female passenger—their faces staring but not staring, eyes looking away but watching me come nearer. The driver tucked in an arm, raised his window, and looked over at his passenger as I stood outside his door.

Understand, I had on my Belmar Beachfront Staff shirt. The patch is white with blue lettering. It's oval, maybe three or four inches long. It's sewn right over the shirt's pocket—a standard, light blue work shirt. I'd even managed to grab my matching blue work cap. Hats, not clothes, make the man.

I leaned down, put my face right up to the driver's window, and mouthed, "You are disturbing my peace."

The driver, about my age, maybe older, with salt and pepper Elvis sideburns and a belly that wanted to nudge his steering wheel, shot me a quick glance before facing front and pulling around the Caddy. The next car followed, and the next, until the intersection was stuffed full of illegal on-the-right passers-by.

Three or four cars bumper to bumper snaked around the Caddy and through the intersection where of course there was no diagonal parking. Too bad Fat Elvis was blocked by the first parked car beyond the intersection and the natural line of traffic he left to pass me.

Then the back-up lights of that first diagonally parked car beyond the intersection flicked on. He backed to within spitting distance of the car ahead of me. I realized that I may never again have an opportunity to create a civic rebellion.

I dashed back to the Caddy, pulled the door shut, and surged ahead to the bumper of the car in front of me. Fat Elvis on my right was blocked by the backing out car, and the backing out car was blocked by me. It was perfect.

When the car in front of me moved, I stayed put to block the backing out car.

Horns started. I couldn't tell where the honks came from because I kept pumping a fist on the Caddy's big chrome blaster. I had the Elvis rhythm down pat.

Soon I had half a block of empty in front of me. I turned and watched Elvis lifting his hands, turning right and left, yelling at his passenger. She put up both hands. They looked as if they were tossing invisible pizzas. The guy trying to back out—someone innocent had to be punished so that justice could strike Fat Elvis—gave up. His back-up lights blinked out, and he pulled forward.

As soon as he pulled ahead, I pulled ahead, right on his bumper so the poor bastard couldn't budge. The Elvis bumper almost touched my right front skirt, and the cars behind him all sat radiator-to-trunk.

I put the Caddy in park and turned her off. I wiggled up on my knees on the front seat, climbed over, and made my way to the back where I sat on the seat top. I lit up a Pall Mall and waved to the people on the boards who had gathered, pointing, and laughing. They waved back.

I felt sorry for the guy in the parked car. He'd pulled so close to the other parked car; he couldn't open his driver-side door. It took him a few minutes to lift himself over his console onto the passenger seat and open that door.

He stood there and opened his arms, regarding first Elvis, and then me. He looked like a nice, elderly gent in his baggy bathing suit and cabana-style top.

I smiled. He stood and looked toward the beach, his elbow on his roof, not caring to face the situation behind him. I wanted Elvis to get out. He kept taking it out on his passenger. He had air conditioning behind closed windows.

In the meantime, cars heading north tried passing the Caddy's left rear fin. They had to cross to the other lane to do it. The traffic coming south, well, they weren't in a giving mood, most of them. Every minute or so, a south-bound Samaritan pulled over to let a north-bound car through. That or they had to stop half a block down to let crossers pass. Those opportunities catapulted the north-bound line forward. Car after car crossed over the double line to get by me until a south-bound driver decided the hell with this and pushed forward. I counted five grill-to-grill stand-offs before the cops arrived.

That wasn't for another several minutes. Maybe they were all uptown. Maybe they were all south of Seaside and couldn't get north. Thanks to me.

Two things moved me from the back seat—one, my ass hurt, and two, I wanted to answer all the horns honking at me. I straddled the front seat. Every time I'd hear a horn—they honked from all around me—I'd lift my arms like a conductor. I had my voice as a stubby baton, and I started to play my horn with my right foot to the famous five notes of The Blue Danube Waltz. Maybe another smart ass would fill in the missing honks.

I honked, bah-dah-dah-dah-dah—and then conducted, dum-dum, dum-dum with my arms. Bah-dah-dah-dah-dah—dum-dum, dum-dum.

Nobody caught on, so I filled in the dum-dums.

Two guys—young, with chains tangling like chicken wire around their necks as they yelled and gestured—gave me shit from their cars. It amazed me no one got out to approach me. I must have looked like I was having too much fun.

"It's flooded," I smiled. I kept conducting with my shiny baton in a cupped palm. I figured if Alice's John Deere neighbor thought it was a gun... Good thing I wasn't in some state where they suckle infants on 30.06s. I imagined the headline: *Man Honking Strauss Shot.*

I couldn't get the damn waltz out of my head. I remembered a cartoon with ducks swimming in time to it. One duck, of course, turned into a swan.

I swayed on my seat to it and kept honking. When I swiveled my left leg over the seat—my testicles weren't exactly comfortable up there—and looked at the boardwalk, there were half a dozen borough workers on the boards laughing their asses off. They clapped and pointed at me.

"Jim-my! Jim-my!"

Turned out they'd been on the beach all day hauling and building a commissioner's brain fart of an idea to make weekend bucks—a temporary Labor Day set-up consisting of refreshment hut and stands for people to sit and watch a volleyball tournament Saturday and Sunday.

I turned the ignition key and found CBS 101.1 oldies on the radio. I had Strauss on the brain.

The Jamies "Summertime, Summertime" came on. It's summertime, summertime, sum-sum summertime. That song came out in 1958 on the way to my high school senior year. I knew all the words.

Well I'm so happy that I could flip/ Oh how I'd like to take a trip/I'm sorry teacher but zip your lip/Because it's summertime

I was mouthing that verse when I heard a siren pulse. A cop car drove the wrong way up Seaside and parked. Now the northbound traffic couldn't turn left to go down Seaside the right way—a grander-scale cluster fuck.

I got down in the seat. I started laughing when I saw Bauer climb out of his cruiser. He looked around, shook his head, and smiled a quick smile that would have made the Cheshire Cat jealous. My six minutes of fame were done.

His grin gone, Bauer snapped, "What the hell's going on, Hanlon?"

"Long story. I tried letting this guy out," I pointed to the diagonally parked, elderly cabana guy, "but I stalled. Then I flooded her. That idiot kept honking," a thumb went back at Fat Elvis. Bauer didn't buy it, but for the whole time I spoke to him, I had the accelerator floored.

"Watch."

Ga-ruu, ga-ruu, ga-ruu, ruu, ruu.

Officer Bauer's partner arrived. He directed traffic flow until a space opened behind me.

"Put it in neutral, Hanlon."

A push back to let out Mr. Cabana-wear followed by a push into his vacated spot, and Ocean Ave jerked into motion.

Bauer checked the meter. "You have almost two hours to get this dinosaur started. Have a nice weekend."

The Caddy's big carbs didn't take that long to clear. She roared to life before I coughed my way through two Pall Malls.

22

THREE BLOCKS LATER I had to wait halfway through Tony Orlando and Dawn—at least I got the chorus of "Summertime, Summertime" out of my head—to turn left.

I parked across the street from Peggy's house. Linda would still be hanging out with her boardwalk buddies. Walking up her front steps, flip-flops slapping with indignation against the wood, I felt like I should be wearing a cop uniform and badge. Justice isn't always timely.

I stopped at her door. I had to laugh remembering Ronny ringing her bell that night, the two of them yelling, Linda yelling, and then the real cops showing up. That's summer—one catchy memory chorus after another that doesn't leave you. They add up and get stored in a three-month jukebox that's always lit up and ready to spin a favorite over the next nine months.

Peggy's big wooden door was open. I knocked on the screen door and rang the bell with the other hand. I had my EL in my pocket. I wanted to sound just as guttural and as harsh as I could. It was no act, either.

Peggy came to the door. "Jimmy," she sighed. She stood with her arms folded. I got the impression she'd had a few. "Well?"

"A quick visit and message. Don't go anywhere near Robin Malloy. If you do, I will knock out your teeth. Don't call; don't visit. Or this," I opened my mouth, smiled, and pointed, "is what your mouth will look like."

I did an about-face and walked to the Caddy. Peggy had never seen me without my partials.

I wouldn't be around after Monday, and I'd never strike a woman, even Peggy. Strangle, maybe, but never strike. Hell, I figured waiting for Peggy to self-destruct was like betting on autumn leaves to fall. Poor Linda. Like I'd told her, she was resilient. It's a good quality to have.

To think I'd had so much fun inside half an hour with only one shot and beer. I headed home, or close to it—I found a spot way down Mercer past C

150

Street—and took a nice long shower. I checked myself in the mirror before it steamed gray. I looked like an old, weather-worn farmer: tanned arms and face, pale torso with flab lines. I'd lost a little weight thanks to cutting down on the booze. My chin skin had thinned and decided to hang closer to my stoma.

I shaved and cleaned up after my shower. I wanted the place to be neat and trim for next week. I almost called the bank since they're open late on Fridays to see if Ronny had deposited my first three hundred dollars. I decided against it. Why inject worry into the weekend?

I walked down to J's. Lipp sat at one of his picnic tables with a cup of coffee. I joined him.

"What the hell are you doing here on a Friday?"

"I thought I might take a chance and eat at your place of business."

"You better go inside. Connie won't serve outside after dusk. She's afraid of mosquitos. Believes they'll infect her with heartworm." Lipp looked ready for his Saturday night bender.

"Isn't that in dogs?"

"Try telling her. I've showed her articles. Tell her when she takes your order."

I went in and ordered a grilled cheese and tomato sandwich. I had a piece of apple pie for dessert. I didn't mention mosquitos to Connie. Listening to her talk about her bunions was bad enough.

Next stop, the Osprey. Not one familiar face. The bar was strictly Benny central. The boys had on their tank tops and shorts and the girls had their tube tops and short shorts. After eight when the dress code changed, they'd return decked out in multi-patterned, smooth-fabric finery.

I stood drinking a bottle of Bud. Either Mr. Kelly had hiked his Labor Day prices a tad, or I wasn't used to the after five o'clock rates. I people watched. Typical Friday evening crowd—tentative but still a little too loud. I didn't see any boy-girl couple whose combined ages would add up to more than a few years past mine.

I walked home after one more beer. Across the parking lot not fifty feet from home, I heard her voice. Peggy rode her daughter's bicycle down the north sidewalk of Mercer, both hands on the handlebars.

"Wait, please."

When I'd heard her, I tensed. Froze might be a better description. No sense fidgeting in front of the firing squad—hold still so it's over quick.

Ten feet from me she stopped and swung her leg back over the seat, dropped the bike and walked up to me. For one crazy moment, I thought she'd kiss me.

"Thank you. Can you help me with this?" she went back to the bike.

"I got it." She was all over the place. She looked like a marionette with half her strings cut.

I walked the bike across to my place and brought it into the vestibule. Peggy followed me up the stairs without saying a word. Her cork-soled shoes clomp-clomped every step.

Inside she kicked them off and collapsed on the sofa. She put her head back over the sofa top and rubbed her temples with both hands.

"I need something."

"How about some coffee?"

She sat forward, leaned her face into her hands, and then shook her hair as if there were bugs in it. "How about you put whiskey in some hot coffee for me."

She turned her head and smiled at me. She really had a nice smile. Her one eye looked a bit to the right when she had a load on.

"You're the boss."

I went out and put the water on to boil. Peggy stood up, walked to the slider, and went out on the balcony. It was dark by then. I saw a match flame and the glow of her cigarette. I followed her out and barely had my ass in a chair when she started talking.

"I don't know how I could have done that. I know why. What a mistake."

"You mean clocking Ronny?"

"This goddamn summer dragged me down." She faced me. Her cigarette shook back and forth between her fingers. "I'm not a bad person. I'd never hit someone. Anyone. I never hit another human being in my life before I smacked that son of a bitch with that bottle. I don't know what the hell came over me. Christ! Amanda Hanks punched me in the nose in fifth grade. I cried and watched her laugh about it."

"Fifth grade, huh?" I had no idea what to say to the woman. I'd threatened to knock her teeth out, and she'd come to visit me.

"It was a mistake. I even blamed Linda. Linda lied to me, yes. But I blamed my daughter, not him! What kind of mother does that?"

She threw her cigarette over the railing and put her face in her hands. Sobs shook her shoulders, and then soft, low moans grew out from under her hands. What a mess. I patted her back every few seconds. After a couple of minutes, she calmed long enough to begin to sniff. She sniffed every few seconds. I checked my pockets. I didn't have my usual bandana. She kept sniffing.

"There's tissues in the bathroom." I started to get up, but she said something stupid.

She sobbed, "I'll get one in a minute. This goddamn balcony. Every time I'm here somebody shits on me."

She'd told Ronny goddamn Sunday. Now it was my goddamn balcony. "Get one now."

She turned in the chair. "Get what?"

"A tissue. Don't lie to yourself."

She raised her head and looked at me. "Lie? Lie about what?"

"Nobody shits on you. You do it to yourself."

"I don't know what the hell you're talking about!"

"Just go get a tissue. Grab a roll of toilet paper. I can't take that sniffing. I know what I'm talking about. I'm talking about lying. It's just self-defense— a wall all around you."

She kept staring at me. I got up and got her the tissues to shut her up. I dropped the box in her lap. "Now you're set. You want a drink? How about something to eat?"

"I can't think about food."

"You'll think about it eventually."

"Are you drunk?"

"I wish. What about the fifth grade? Tell me about this Hanks girl. Why'd she punch you?"

She blew her nose. Now that she'd stopped blubbering, she looked very attractive in the light coming from the pole in the center of the Osprey parking lot across the street.

"I don't remember."

"You remember."

"Boyfriend stuff," she chuckled.

"Why didn't you hit her back?"

"Shit, I don't know."

"I'd like to think you'd hit her back. I can picture you doing it. Did your nose bleed?"

"She didn't punch me in the nose. She had a lot of friends with her. What did you mean about me lying?"

"You wanted something you knew you couldn't have. Ronny told me what you said about you two—that you were doomed from the start. You wanted his money; you wanted a truck. You wanted."

"I don't know," she sighed. "I won't say anything to that girl. You think I will? Otherwise, you wouldn't have threatened me." She smiled at me. "I'll knock your teeth out you said. Do you believe me? That I'll leave them both alone?"

"I believe you'll fetch the sheriff, rustle up a posse, and string up Ronny over the branch of an oak tree."

"Hah! At least I'm not the only nut case on this balcony. I don't suppose you're going to knock my teeth out anymore."

"No, I have to work tomorrow. Remember "Batman" on TV? All those big words when somebody got hit. Bang, boom, and splat. I wonder what sound your teeth would make?"

"Crunch? No, crack! Depending on what they got hit with. Since you're up—how about two of your famous screwdrivers?"

"I'm way overdue."

I went in and fixed them. I put about two drops of vodka in Peggy's. When I came back, she was about to light a cigarette. She smoked Winstons. I put down the drinks, took my Pall Malls out from my pocket, and shook some out from the pack for her. I never opened the entire top wrapper on cigarettes—only one side of the stamp. It took a few shakes.

"Try one of these."

"Thanks," she took one. "Non-filters, the real deal. Matter which end?"

"Some smoke the ink, some suck it." I showed her what I meant—the Pall Mall lettering and insignia at one end. I read her the slogan on the pack, "Wherever particular people congregate." I lit it for her.

"Thank you," she picked up her drink. "Cheers. To one crazy summer."

I sat down, and we clinked glasses. "One and the same."

We sat with our drinks watching the comings and goings along Ocean Ave. By our third drink—Peggy chugged her first, and I figured what the hell and made her other two normal—we weren't talking much.

She or I would comment on something—a loud car stereo, people chugging beers in the parking lot. She went inside twice to pee.

I think she passed out for a few minutes. Her head drooped. I watched her breathing. When she woke up, she shook her head, rubbed her face, and I think slurred, "All these goddamn people. Go home."

"What? Wake up!"

"Shit!"

"Everybody goes home!" I waved.

She pulled herself up with the aid of the railing. "It's time. Shit," she steadied herself.

"Nope. You'll get arrested for drunk pedaling. You're sleeping here."

She put her head back and laughed. Arms out straight, hands griping the railing, she howled, "Me sleeping with a gay man."

"How about that?" She let me guide her inside. I steered us both to the spare room. "You sleep here. This is Ronny's old room."

"So what?" she laughed. "Big deal." She took one more step and then spun around in my arms. Our faces almost touched. "Think he'll be back tonight?"

"Who knows?"

Sad smile locked in place, her eyes searched around me as if she was willing him to appear in the doorway behind us. I took her elbows and sat her down on the bed. I sat next to her. Sure. Ronny and Robin. They'll both be along for us any second now.

I watched her settle down. I put a blanket over her before heading back to the balcony where I took the bone I'd rolled out of my shirt pocket and fired it up.

The traffic moved at a good clip now. The boards looked deserted—not more than a few people. Travelers and locals had settled in doing whatever the hell sane people did on the first day of Labor Day weekend. Peggy and I settled in.

That was the biggest lie of all.

23

NEWGRANGE DATES TO approximately 3,200 BC. It's an ancient temple and passage tomb in Ireland's Boyne Valley, and older than both Stonehenge and the Great Pyramid of Giza. Built about 2,500 years before the Celts, the mound covers about one acre. It's known for the rising sun of the winter solstice penetrating an opening in the roof and lighting the floor of Newgrange's passage and chamber. You can play a lottery for free to win a chance to stand in the passage as the ancients stood at dawn on the mornings of December 19th to the 23rd. By this marking of the end of the longest night of the year, some believe the great mound represents a victory of life over death. Warmth will soon return. Crops will again grow.

I felt plenty of warmth Labor Day Saturday. I got cooked. It felt more like July than September. My umbrella didn't help. All afternoon the west breeze blew heat off the Ocean Ave blacktop.

They assigned me to a gate for the entire day. The regular gate guard quit. The borough had to come up with a couple of emergency fill-ins—two guys from the DPW became gate guards. That might not sound difficult, but when you're used to dealing with tree limbs or cutting grass and suddenly find yourself face to face with a vacationing horde, things might get dicey.

Man, it was busy. I saw so many day tickets and badges. Labor Day is like church on Easter or Christmas. Some people who never show up other days feel some need to show up on the biggies.

I took my break after Bob left. I walked across the street to the Engine Room. Banned though I was, I figured there would be a different bartender working. I thought about taking off my work shirt and having a couple of beers. I did. I sat there on a sunny day in my sleeveless T, tan lines above the elbows, then white from mid-bicep to bare shoulder. I didn't give a shit.

For my dining pleasure, I stuck in a quarter in the lobby snack machine, pulled a knob, and ate a pack of peanut butter crackers. For an hour, I drank and watched the bartender clean and wipe down glassware and shelves. I didn't know him. He didn't know me.

At five as I packed up, the sand still vibrated with the crowd. I pictured a black and white photo of the scene—a postcard of Coney Island from the twenties except for the beach fashions.

My walk home took forever. Even the guards stowing their equipment in the storage bins looked beat. I didn't see any red Belmar sweats in Estel's front window when I walked past. The line to get in snaked down from the porch steps damn near to the sidewalk. All I wanted was a cool shower and a tall cocktail.

At home I made the mistake of blasting the AC and camping out on the couch. A few hours later, a racket of knocking and voices woke me up.

I went out onto the balcony. Long shadows announcing twilight stretched down Mercer.

"Who is it?" I called down.

Nothing. I recognized the voices between the knocks. I went inside, filled a glass from the bathroom, came back out and poured it onto the walk. Ronny stuck his head out and smiled up at me.

"Is that a new burglar alarm?"

"I pee in this cup and leave it out here for just such occasions."

The Bronx toady emerged. "Jim—ee."

"Come on," Ronny looked up, "we're taking you out. One last summer night."

"Robin coming?"

"Boy's night out."

"I'm beat. I don't think I could go out if you loaded my ass into a giant catapult and zinged me one block to the Osprey. Can't do it." A truck with a muffler the size of an oil drum roared past. "Hold on," I held up a finger.

I went down and unlocked my door.

"Who are you afraid of?" Ronny said in passing. Vinny followed him up. I imitated a suit of armour watching them climb my stairs.

In the living room, I said, "I'll smoke a bone with you." I shrugged. "I just woke up. Haven't had a shower or dinner."

"Come out with us. One more summer night."

"Summer's over."

"Another's coming. You'll remember this one."

I had papers and mixings spread on an album cover. "Would you like to continue this pointless conversation or watch me roll a bone?" I put down my voice, pinched the paper, and went to work.

I lit up, and we passed it. The smoke lifted in thick clouds before swirling in the air around the AC vent. After we finished, we sat around as if we'd just eaten a big meal. Ronny went over to the record player and started looking through my albums.

"What do you want to hear?" Ronny slid aside one album for another.

"Pick one. I'm taking a shower."

"Hey," Ronny called, "I put in two months' worth of rent. We're good until Halloween."

"Great."

Vinny looked restless. Good. I counted on him to get Ronny out of there. I took as long as I could in the bathroom. I bet I used every ounce of hot water in the condo. I came out with a towel wrapped around me. The TV had a stupid game show on. They were gone. I got dressed and made myself a drink.

I sat on the balcony and thought about what would happen in Jersey after Labor Day. We'd put up snow fences and plant sea oats to preserve our beach. Bulldozers would pile up mounds of sand to protect the boardwalk. Shutters would cover the mini-golf ticket windows. Standing signs that promised discounts and sales would get stored away to wait for a new paint job with next year's price hikes. Estel's marquee would lose letters and lights. Padlocks would snap closed on Mrs. G's office and Mr. and Mrs. P's snack bar. Parking meters would lose their heads. The Lipp would batten down J's.

Newgrange was built five thousand years ago. That's less than a spit in history's ocean. Compared to Newgrange, Labor Day is a brand-new blip on antiquity's radar—a billboard to divert us along our annual journey around the sun. After Labor Day, steer straight for a B&B and fall foliage. Caution: only forty-seven shopping days until Christmas. Head left after New Year's and— Super Bowl! A quick right into Valentine's Day, and then a detour for a Spring Clearance on all mattresses, box springs, sheets, pillows, and pads in stock. Next bear right for Easter/ Passover and buy now to receive $500 cash-back or interest-free payments for 48 months with no money down and don't forget Mom this Mother's Day.

The only similarity between Newgrange and Labor Day is this—at Newgrange, even if you win the lottery, you can't count on bright sunshine to illuminate the passage. The same goes for summer weekends in Jersey. Overnight, some kind of nasty cold front smacked right into us.

24

IT POURED SUNDAY. Rain, a chilled rain—at times I couldn't see drops, just sheets—ran down streets, swelled over curbs, and pooled around sewer drains choked with early leaves. Cars didn't swoosh by; they eased along through flooded streets like tip-toeing old ladies. From under my umbrella, I watched dresses lifting knee high, garbage bag rain gear, towels over heads—all manner of ridiculous efforts to keep some body part dry. When I saw two girls splashing next to the clogged drain across the boards from my gate, I gave them a nice hand.

The rain let up before noon. A few light patches of sky showed through the clouds now and then. People started coming out of sidewalk cracks with kid wagons, coolers, and beach chairs. They should have checked with Uncle Wethbee. Even though he's dead he could have told them the rain wasn't going anywhere.

I don't know why I thought of Uncle Wethbee, the former TV weatherman. The schmuck got himself fired maybe ten years ago. A news story about a rape ran before his weather report and he made a crazy comment, something like, remember the words of Confucius, if rape is inevitable, lie back and enjoy it. I sat back, shivering in my blanket, and enjoyed the spectacle of people willing themselves to ignore hypothermia.

A family of eight came to my gate—at least I'd gotten assigned to Pine instead of Monmouth. They lined up like a mother duck with ducklings, except Papa led the way. He pulled a jumbo kid's wagon loaded with a big cooler, at least four umbrellas, and topped it off with sand chairs. His wife followed, and then came the kids, from youngest to oldest. Every one of them had red hair.

The father flashed me three adult daily badges. "I see my spot."

He and the woman took off down the ramp leaving the kids behind. His spot? The beach looked like *Lawrence of Arabia* without Arabs.

161

The oldest kid brought up the rear—an only daughter in her teens. She treated her four brothers like sheep. The boys acted as if she had a Nazi arm band and a Luger. None of them looked at me as she herded them along, faces staring at the crematorium dead ahead.

"Show the man your badge," she instructed each as he passed.

"Want one, pal?" I offered each one a Blow-Pop.

The daughter said, "Say no, thank you." Each boy repeated the phrase.

"You may have one," I held out a pop for her as she came by.

She smiled at me, "No, thank you."

"Let's go!" the father yelled from his spot.

The second his feet left the ramp and touched sand, each boy took off in a jog. Running heads down, small arms pumping, they made their way to their father while their sister stopped to take off her flip-flops.

Dad erected a small umbrella city. As the rain let up, he had the boys out from under and in line. He led them in jumping jacks and some toe-touching before his arm swept forward like Moses' staff ordering everybody to the water. Older sister got to stay undercover to make lunch.

It's Labor Day weekend—never mind the cold rain. We're having fun, damnit. We saw the billboard.

Americans worship at many alters. All too often, we kneel before our summer mirrors. We won't stare into it—just a glimpse in passing to catch the glitter and sparkle—to picture ourselves winning the lottery, driving that new car, telling the boss to piss off. We forget that it's a funhouse mirror. It distorts. It needs a warning—*Reflections which cause heartache may not be visible*. We wouldn't read it. Instead we tarry in our own personal amusement parks, beguiled by dreams long after all the rides have shut down, and all the lights have blinked dark.

When the boys got back, under the umbrellas they tore into the sandwiches Sis handed out. I wondered if the old man was going to make them wait half an hour before going back in the water the way Dad did. He had his unwritten rules like anyone else. I wondered again what he would have thought if Mother had revealed my secret. Maybe she thought it would shatter his summer mirror. It had surely cracked when Teresa was discovered. How many times in his mind's eye did Sean watch his curveball fool one big league batter after another? And when they waited on it—swoosh! He blew that fastball right past them.

I thought about what I'd say and do Monday at Alice's. I wasn't up for getting anointed as my son-in-law's symbol of evil. I'd had it with juvenile bullshit. My summer with a laryngectomy had taught me that too many people never really leave the schoolyard.

Summer ended in the rain that Sunday. It turned down the radio volume, pulled over to the boardwalk, lowered the top, and rolled up the windows after flicking a cigarette into the street. It turned off the ignition. The wipers stopped in mid-thump, and as the windshield spotted with rain, rivulets rolled in crooked trails. Through the fogged glass, there wasn't a single jogger, bike rider, or walker in sight.

Work on Labor Day was a church belch, a warm beer, cold pizza left in the box on top of the oven overnight. The sky never made up its mind—clear, rain, or cloudy.

After work, Annie caught me in time to give me the quilt—my last summer surprise.

I held it up with both hands before presenting it back to her so I could speak. At first, I couldn't find words.

"Annie, you're the best. I love what you did with his name."

She had done much more work than I'd asked. She had affixed a stream-shaped, light blue material and then sewn Antony's name on top. It gave the letters movement and life. She had trees and rocks around the stream—all kinds of extras that really made the quilt look peaceful.

"What do I owe you?"

"What did we say?" she huffed. "That's what you owe me."

"But Annie—"

"Not a penny more."

I slipped in an extra twenty.

"I'm off to Red Bank. Let me know when you make Italian again. You have fun at your daughter's today," she called back as she walked away.

I dropped the quilt off at Denny's. He wasn't home. He has a small porch with a few chairs. I covered it up with my official borough outer ware, left a note to Denny on top, and headed home to change. The note was from a Thoreau quote—*Launch yourself on every wave.*

By the time I got home, cleaned up and changed, it was six o'clock. On the way to Sea Girt along Ocean Ave, people surrendered to the inevitable. Trunks and bars packed, families loaded into minivans, fathers hurried grumpy kids. I had my polished pewter flask filled with good whiskey—didn't want to disappoint my host.

I parked and killed the ignition across the street from Alice's to look over the plantings. Everything looked nice. I checked myself in the rearview. I tested my voice—the shiny piece of undulating buzz I'd wanted to throw away a thousand times. It took the summer, but I found my voice.

I didn't realize Alice and the girls had crossed the street until they stood in its middle. I popped the handle on my door. The street's bowing made it hard to open.

"Here, I'll help," Alice said. She let go of Suzanne's hand to grab the door handle. Jessica had other ideas. "You have it, Dad? Jessica!"

The child didn't want any part of the Caddy, me, or her mother. She tried to pull her hand from her mother's. She dug her heels in and pulled back. One of her little flip-flops came loose.

I pushed the door open. Good thing it was a side street—there was no traffic.

"Pop-pop!" Suzanne said.

I let the door swing closed by itself and knelt. "Hello, Miss Suzanne."

"Jessica, stop!"

Dad came to the rescue. "You shouldn't have them out in the street, Alice." He picked up Jessica.

"Fip-fop," she pointed down at her lost pink footwear.

"Hello, Bill."

"James. Left your student home I see."

"She could teach you a few things." We all crossed to the yard.

Suzanne held her mother's hand and skipped to the back door. Bill unloaded his youngest with, "Go play on your swing set." Then, "Everybody, this is James, Alice's father."

One dozen pairs of eyes checked me out from folding yard chairs. I smiled and raised my hello hand. A radio on a picnic table played elevator music.

"Very nice to see all of you." Probably three of them heard me. A few smiled before going back to their conversations. From what I could tell, cocktail hour hadn't graduated into chow time.

Then Sophie stood up. I caught the movement from the corner of my eye and knew at once who it was—the way she gripped the chair arms, tilted forward, and then stood straight and tall as if permitting cameras to focus before she took her first step.

"Hello, Jimmy."

I walked to her. "Excuse my voice, Sophie."

"Don't be silly," she hummed.

She spread her arms, and I filled them. A couple of pats later, she took hold of my shoulders and guided me half a step back.

"You look terrific."

"Thank you. Always the charmer." She held her hand out towards Alice. "Our little girl with two of her own."

I couldn't take my eyes off her. She looked like Sophie, all right. But her formal manner and speech were her mother's.

"Our little girl has grown up." I looked up at the sky and cast out my line. "It's a precious day for a picnic."

"Yes, yes, it is. A precious family day."

Bait taken, I reeled in. "To family," I whipped out my flask. I took a gentleman's sip, tucked away my flask, and smiled as wide as my partials allowed.

Sophie made her old you-puked-on-a-tree face. I took her elbow.

"Family first. Your chair, m'dear."

I didn't ask Sophie why hubby Stan wasn't with her. She'd go home to him. He got to keep the prize, so I didn't concern myself.

I wandered over to the deluxe swing/playhouse/slide where Jessica and Suzanne were playing. Alice came alongside me and handed me a cold can of Bud. She gave me a shoulder squeeze.

"Thanks so much for coming. I know you had a busy weekend."

"Thanks for asking me. I need to talk to you."

You would have thought I'd just told her about Pearl Harbor.

"Oh, Dad. I have to get these people fed, feed the girls," she dropped her hands. I took hold of one.

"It's not about what you think. I'm taking a trip, that's all. I've sublet the condo."

Her face relaxed. "A trip? Where to?"

"Ireland."

"Oh my gosh! That sounds great, Dad." She hugged me. "When? Where? You have to tell me all about it."

"Tomorrow, as a matter of fact. I'm flying out of Newark. Got my ride all set."

She looked at me. I saw a thousand questions in her eyes. Then her head jerked around.

"Jessica…Suzanne, don't move! Stay there, Suzanne!"

Alice zipped over to the slide. Jessica stood grinning at the bottom with her arms spread, ready to catch her sister. Suzanne sat at the top with a smile that reminded me of a certain lifeguard.

"Alice, I'm starting the grill," Bill called from across the yard.

Bill had his chicken ready to go. He'd par-boiled it. It sat steaming in a big pot. He tonged it one piece at a time onto his gas grill. I stood by to watch. He put the breasts alongside each other, the thighs and drumsticks across from the breasts. He wore a big white apron that looped around his neck and tied in the back.

"Looks like you're setting up troops," I pointed.

"The secret's the heat differential on either side. The breasts still have a bit of cooking to do. The thighs and drumsticks are set. Take over for me?" he held up the tongs.

I took his weapon. "Do my best."

"There's really nothing to do."

He took a pad and pencil from his shirt pocket and made the rounds, stopping, asking, and writing at each lawn chair, starting with his mother-in-law. He was right. I had nothing to do. I still poked at a few breasts.

"Okay," Bill said when he returned. "Still like to help?"

"Nothing I'd like more. Here," I handed him the tongs, took out my flask, and took a gentleman's sip. "It cuts the smoke," I smiled after I tucked the flask away.

"What is that?"

"It's better than what your guests are drinking."

Bill stood there holding the tongs along with his pad. He held it out to me. "Okay. All you need to do is a little math. Read me how many thighs, legs, and breasts I need with barbeque sauce."

I looked at his pad. "Does B stand for breast?"

"L for leg, T for thigh. You got it." He clicked the ends of the tongs together three times. He dangled the loop end from two fingers and twirled the tongs.

"So B slash S stands for breast with sauce."

"What I did was ask every chair what they wanted. If somebody said two thighs with barbeque sauce, I wrote 2T slash S. 2T is two thighs without sauce."

I kept staring at the pad. "So you didn't write 2T small s for plural."

"S is for sauce."

"I see."

"Got it now? Hey, you don't have to do this. I don't want to put you out," he held his hands apart. "I just thought you might like to get involved with family activities."

"I'm grateful. A man doesn't get an opportunity to see his daughter and grandchildren every day."

Bill showed me his back and started turning chicken. Alice came by with seasoned salt, lemon pepper, and a shaky bottle of something. She put everything down on the grill's side counter.

"What's in the bottle, honey?"

"Mostly vinegar with melted butter and spices. All good flavors," Alice mused.

"Secret recipe?"

"Kind of," she smiled. "Everything alright?"

"We're getting there, aren't we, Bill?"

He turned one leg at a time. He didn't roll them; he picked up each one and turned it so the bone end faced north when it had previously faced south.

"I have to take drink orders," Alice hurried off.

"I'll order one." I tossed Bill's pad onto the grill counter, took out my flask, and sipped. I smacked my lips.

"Damnit!" Bill huffed. He put down the tongs and picked up the pad. A grease spot spread across the paper. Bill sprinkled a secret recipe all over the chicken. Smoke rose as flames hissed and licked up. After shaking seasoned salt and lemon pepper, he picked up the brush from the bowl holding red barbeque sauce. Reading from the pad, he started dabbing sauce onto the chicken.

"I'd still like to help."

"Go chug your flask."

He finished dabbing, put down the brush, and lined up all the red sauce pieces opposite from the naked, secret recipe pieces.

"Red breasts, legs, and thighs all together on the cooler side. Am I right?"

He poked at a breast. It spit a sizzle.

"Still like your new plantings?"

"Yes."

"The perennials won't show much right away. You'll get more and more flowers each year. You know what they say. First year sleep, second year creep, third year leap. They're like people. You must look years down the road to see how beautiful they might become."

"I told you. I like and appreciate your efforts. I believe they were sincere."

"That's a funny word to use with your back turned."

"What's that?"

"Sincere. I said it's a funny word to—"

"I heard you."

"I can never tell with this gizzmo if somebody hears me or not. You always have trouble hearing me over the phone."

"When you call. If you're sober enough to call." He clicked his tongs. "At least you didn't bring that so-called student along. It's still a mistake having you here."

That closed the book for me on eejits, as they say in Ireland, like my son-in-law. I even gave the bastard the last word, but I had the last smile.

I went inside to find Alice. Schlepping with drinks, she had her nose going back and forth from booze bottles to a drink order note pad.

"Is that note pad your idea or Bill's?" I laughed.

"The pad and idea are both his."

"You don't know bourbon from Budweiser. You take these made ones out. I'll get the rest."

I fixed up drinks so that no one would need a refill until next Friday. Then I ducked out the front door to the car to get my file folder with all the papers Alice would need. I left it in the girls' bedroom on their dresser where neither could reach it. I wasn't sure, but I doubted the only time Bill went in the girls' room was when he installed or removed the window screen.

I went back out, found a vacant chair, and sat down to wait for dinner. Alice had the girls fed and in the tub by the time Generalissimo had his chicken battalion ready for duty. I kept my flask between my legs next to my dinner plate, waiting for Bill to glance over. He never did.

I gave myself ten minutes after I ate before I stood up, chucked my plate in the garbage, and started my goodbyes. I only had four. Sophie was first.

"We made a great daughter," I told her, "and she made beautiful granddaughters."

I went inside. I found Alice toweling the girls, all pink and fragrant from their tub, giggling blooms with one-piece bathing suit tans.

"Good night, honey. I got a date tomorrow with a ticket agent."

"Can you wait, Dad? I just have to put the girls in bed and read them their story."

"It's been a nice night. Give me a squeeze. I'll send lots of postcards."

"Promise? I want lots and lots."

"I promise." The girls were next. Suzanne accidently covered my stoma and cut off my air. Jessica gave me a sideways look before she did a quick arm lock around my bent knee.

"There's a folder I left on the girls' dresser, honey. Papers and legal stuff."

My daughter knelt on the floor with my grandchildren. She looked up at me.

"Planes can go splash."

"Oh, Dad," she pooh-poohed. She hoisted up Jessica, took Suzanne's hand, and the four of us parted amid staccato good nights.

I drove home through the thinning traffic. Parking the Caddy—I found a nice spot right in front of my place—I remembered it was my anniversary. One year ago on Labor Day, or somewhere close, I had my laryngectomy.

It bought time for this summer.

Next morning, already packed, I left the door unlocked and the keys to the condo and Caddy on the table next to my CB radio. I wrote Ronny three letters but ripped up each one.

At the door, waiting for the guy I hired to drive me to Newark, I had a thought. I went back inside, wrote Ronny a note after all, and stuck it inside the freezer. *Dear Swan Shooter*, it read. *If you're looking for ice, okay. If you're looking for my stash, tough shit. I took it with me—the expedient thing to do.*

I hope he laughed when he read it, with Robin laughing right alongside.

25

RUINS OF ANCIENT ring forts dot the land on the Dingle Peninsula in County Kerry. These were places for refuge, storage, or livestock enclosure. There are hundreds of them. At many, a hole in the ground leads to underground passages. Archaeologists call this a souterrain. Some believe these ancient tunnels and chambers are home to fairies and underground castles, and some believe Saint Brendon sailed from Mt. Brandon's base, and Saint Patrick spread the word. This is Ireland, where the tangible, mystical, and mythical all cross paths. To spare a fairy tree—better known as a hawthorn—the Irish will happily spend more time and money to build a road around the living tree rather than cut it down to make way for new pavement.

I stand near Dunquin, Ireland's western most settlement, and gaze west. With time and distance fondness grows, nostalgia fades, and sentiment surrenders to necessity. I walk and listen to the sea and watch stars pop from the night sky like a run of blues knifing the surface. Gusts paw my hat. Tweed is wonderful. Clouds float along in ghostly layers, but as they part and let sunshine strike green—shades and layers of it—I look beyond the blue water and feel the Blaskets open their arms. I feel I'll make spring, see the flora on the Burren, and climb Mt. Brandon. The wind and waves that batter this peninsula I know only in part, and I'm happy to learn wherever I wander until like an old elephant, it's time to return home.

THE END

About the Author

Mick Bennett is from Belmar, New Jersey. Bennett attended Gettysburg College, and after graduation in 1975, found a job at a high school 15 miles from Gettysburg where he taught for 33 years. Bennett is the author of: *Take the Lively Air, Missing You in Belmar, Summer Mirrors, Boardwalk Man,* and *Beat the Blues.*